CHRYSTAL FALLS 2

BREAKING THE RULES

Candice F. Ransom

SCHOLASTIC INC.
New York Toronto London Auckland Sydney

ISBN 0-590-33761-0

12 11 10 9 8 7 6 5 4 3 2 1   10   5 6 7 8 9/8 0/9

CHRYSTAL FALLS 2

BREAKING THE RULES

CHRYSTAL FALLS

Chapter One

She couldn't find the other earring. No matter how desperately she went through the top section of her jewelry box, the tiny gold love knot eluded her fingers.

Mitch gave me those earrings for my birthday, Karen Pickett thought. I *can't* have lost one.

It wasn't just the missing earring. Everything that could possibly go wrong this evening, had.

It's this stupid date, Karen rationalized, almost sick to her stomach with misgivings. I shouldn't have let Dawn talk me into it.

Bad luck apparently ruled Karen's life this evening.

The navy shirt she'd first put on had an unmistakable chocolate stain on one sleeve, forcing her to wear the soft rose sweater that her mother had found on sale. Preferring earthy colors, Karen shied away from the frivolous pink sweater until the Hershey bar decided the issue. Pushing the angora sleeves up to her elbows, she had to admit her mother was right — this shade of pink did look wonderful with her dark eyes and hair.

Her hair! That was *another* problem. Ordinarily Karen washed it, blew it dry until it fell softly to her shoulders, and forgot about it. Complicated hairstyles were definitely not for her. In gym she could pull her hair back in a ponytail, not to be bothered. But tonight she wanted something beyond her old wash-and-wear style and had fiddled with a pair of tortoiseshell combs for almost twenty minutes, before throwing them across the room. However disciplined she might be on the volleyball court, her hair was completely untrainable.

The list went on. Her cat Horatio had gotten into a fight with the neighbor's dog and limped home that afternoon with a torn ear. Karen's mother was slamming around in the kitchen, fuming over the anticipated vet bill and the fact that Karen's father was late coming home from work.

And now Karen had lost one of her precious earrings.

Why did I ever agree to this date? Karen asked herself miserably, carrying her jewelry box over to the window where there was better light. I must have been out of my mind.

Dawn had arranged the whole thing. A triple date. Dinner at the country club. Dawn and Ian MacFarland, Karen and Mitch, the insufferable Chelsea Chrystal and her snob of a boyfriend, Ryan.

"If we all just sat down and spent an evening together, we'd find out that we really aren't so different," Dawn had said. "Try it, Karen. Please. Just this once."

"What about Chelsea?" Karen had countered. "Is she going to try?"

"I haven't asked her yet," Dawn admitted. "But you know Chelsea —"

Yes, she did. Anything for excitement, that was Chelsea Chrystal . . . Princess Chelsea.

In theory, it sounded innocent enough. Three couples going out to dinner. A pleasant evening? But how could that be, with all the bad feelings between Karen and Chelsea? When Karen was totally honest, she had to admit most of the bad feeling came from her, just because she was Mill and Chelsea was Hill. Chelsea couldn't help being the princess of Chrystal Falls, the beautiful rich girl who had it all. Then came that awful time when the whole town turned against Mitch, who had been wrongly accused of injuring a young Hill boy in a hit-and-run accident. Karen's heart pounded every time she thought about those nightmare days, with Mitch in jail and Miles Fairchild deep in a coma. If the boy had died, Mitch could have been tried for manslaughter . . . but Miles recovered, and Mitch had been exonerated. But the harsh words and accusations about Mitch and milltowners lingered in Chrystal Falls still, like a bad taste. And the incident had made Karen more antagonistic toward Chesea.

Because she liked Dawn, Karen reluctantly had agreed to go on this date.

Just after school began, Dawn Newhouse had moved to Chrystal Falls with her older brother Josh and her mother, who was a doctor at the hospital. Gossip raced through small towns and Chrystal Falls was no exception. Karen quickly learned that Dr. Walter Gilbert was Dawn's uncle, and he had helped the Newhouse family relocate after the death of Dawn's father.

Dawn had come into Chrystal Falls with an open mind, eager to be friends with anyone. It wasn't her fault she walked into a hornet's nest. Even though Dawn knew now that mill-towners like Karen and Mitch never mixed with Chelsea and Ryan's set — the rich, Mercedes-in-every-garage group who lived on the Hill — Dawn refused to take sides. Not even when Mitch was in jail and everyone it seemed, except Karen, believed he had run over an innocent child. Dawn was that kind of person.

Karen tilted the jewelry case to catch the late afternoon light. The box was a hand-me-down from her mother. "You need something to keep your things in," Mrs. Pickett had said last summer after Mitch had given Karen the love-knot earrings. "Take my old one."

Karen knew her mother had kept the old jewelry box for years, since she was Karen's age, sixteen. It was a leather box, with a fleur-de-lis pattern stamped in gold on the worn lid. The top opened to reveal a pop-up tray lined with stiff red satin and divided into sections to hold smaller items. Karen didn't care much for jewelry. When her mother gave her the box, she threw the few pieces she owned into the tray, without even looking in the bottom part.

She had to find that other earring. How could she have been so careless? She hated to think of Mitch scraping together that much money to spend on her.

Karen pulled out a Woolworth's birthstone bracelet set with fake alexandrite hearts. One of the charms was inscribed with "June." Johnny's Christmas present to her when he was eleven. Karen had worn it all that day, never reminding her older brother that her birthday was in July.

A trip down Memory Lane was not finding the earring, though. She tossed the bracelet back in the box and reached into the bottom section, bringing out a tangle of chains. Something was snarled among the junk necklaces — a pin. Karen had never seen it before.

She worked it free and held it in her palm. The pin was shaped like an emblem, enameled in burgundy and gold with a tiny cougar in the center. Across the top the year "1960" was worked in gold. It seemed to be some sort of school pin. She recognized the colors of Chrystal Falls High, and the Chrystal Falls Cougars were the best football team in the county. Had her mother received this pin as an award or something?

Karen was puzzled, but she didn't have time to ask her mother about it. Spotting her missing earring in the corner of the jewelry box, she slipped it into her pierced ear just as Mitch's car horn blared outside. She raced out the door, calling to her mother when she'd be home.

Karen winced inwardly, as she did every time she saw the red car idling in front of the Pickett's house. A child had been struck by that car — if he had died, the vehicle would have been declared a lethal weapon. After the accident, even though Mitch had *not* been the driver, he had wanted to get rid of the car, but it was paid for and ran like a Cadillac, thanks to his expert maintenance. "I can't afford another car anyway," Mitch had said. Though he had hammered out the dents and replaced the grill, Karen couldn't help feeling a twinge whenever he picked her up.

Mitch leaned over to open the door for her. "I don't know why I ever let you talk me into this," he said grimly, as she slid in to sit close to him. "I can think of five dozen things I'd rather be doing tonight than eating with Miss Chrystal Falls and Ryan the Simp. Like asphalting a driveway or digging a well." Mitch had always despised Ryan Simpson and there had never been any great love lost between him and Chelsea, either.

He didn't even notice my new sweater,

Karen thought. The evening was already off to a dismal start.

Passing through the gates of the Chrystal Falls Country Club presented another obstacle. The guard on duty took one look at Mitch's beat-up car and asked for their passes in a tone that clearly indicated he thought they belonged in a demolition derby, not this members-only club.

Mitch had worked at the club for three years, until the accident last month, repairing lawn mowers and other machinery. When he was thrown in jail, the country club let him go. After Mitch was cleared, he was offered his old job again, but even if they raised his salary to a thousand dollars a week, Mitch said, he'd never go back. Now he worked after school and on weekends at a garage.

The guard still wouldn't let them pass. Mitch hit the steering wheel with his fist. "For three years, they let me in to fix golf carts. When I want to eat dinner here, I'm suddenly not good enough."

Karen spoke up, before Mitch said something he shouldn't. "We're meeting friends for dinner," she addressed the attendant.

"You have reservations?" The guard produced a clipboard with a flourish.

"I'll say," Mitch muttered under his breath.

"Look under Chrystal," Karen supplied.

"The magic word," Mitch said when the gates were released, permitting them to drive through. "I didn't know whether to tip that character or get out and salaam at his feet."

Karen looked at Mitch and they both laughed. He leaned over and kissed her cheek. "What the hell. It's only one night."

The others were already there, seated at a table near a window overlooking the golf course, the clipped greens now shrouded in dusky, autumn shadows. Music boomed from a concert-quality stereo system. The laughter that came from the crowded tables seemed forced to Karen, who was suddenly overwhelmed by the lavish decor. And this was only the grill room!

"You're late," Chelsea said by way of greeting. "I was afraid you weren't coming." For Chelsea, this night was different, and Chelsea was always looking for something out of the ordinary.

When the High Princess commands, the peasants had better hustle to Court, Karen thought wryly.

Mitch held out a captain's chair for Karen. "It took us a little while to get here. We don't exactly live right next door, you know."

Dawn broke in, quickly. "It doesn't matter. We haven't been waiting long, really." She looked pointedly at Ian, who sipped a half-finished Coke, as if urging him to fill the awkward silence that fell over the table.

"Good to see you again," Ian said smoothly, following Dawn's lead.

"It's been ages," Ryan remarked. "Since sixth period."

The red-aproned waiter rescued the moment, pouring ice water into glasses and handing menus around. Karen leaned over to compliment Dawn on her outfit — she looked especially cute this evening in black cropped pants and an over-sized, zippered shirt.

"What about me?" Chelsea asked, smiling. "Aren't I cute, too?"

Actually, Chelsea looked smashing in a purple suede miniskirt that revealed miles of legs sheathed in fishnet stockings. Her ankles were crossed casually, showing off butter-soft leather boots that Karen suspected cost more than her own father earned in an entire week.

Catching Dawn's pleading glance, Karen said reluctantly, "You look okay."

"My sister Amy has a sweater just like yours," Chelsea said to Karen, trying to say something pleasant. Chelsea was a Chrystal, but she was never deliberately nasty.

Karen, however, thought Chelsea was implying that her outfit was babyish and was silent. As she opened her menu, she consoled herself with the fact that her gray flannel slacks were a size five and, although she had bought the pants half-price at Godine's, they fit perfectly. Chelsea had a terrific figure, too, but she hadn't been a size five since she was in fifth grade, Karen was certain.

Beside her, Mitch tensed and Karen knew why. "Six ninety-five for a hamburger!" she exclaimed. "A dollar fifty for a Coke."

Ryan Simpson was peering at her over the edge of his menu. "Too rich for your blood?"

Embarrassment washed over Karen in a scarlet wave. How could she have been so stupid? True, they were sitting in the grill room of the country club rather than the formal dining room. But how could she have thought hamburgers and french fries would be cheap? Even worse, she had humiliated Mitch, implying to the others that he couldn't afford to pay these prices.

"I was just — reading out loud," Karen said, trying to hide her blunder.

Ryan wouldn't leave it alone. He said to Mitch, "If you're short of cash, Boyd, I can cover you."

Mitch glared back. "I've got plenty. Lay off, will you?"

"How's the spaghetti here?" Dawn said hurriedly. "Passable?"

"Messy," Chelsea replied with a smile. Then she asked, "Does anybody have the time?"

What a peculiar question, Karen thought, noting the expensive gold watch strapped to Chelsea's slender wrist, but that was Chelsea. Never do anything for yourself someone can do for you.

The waiter was back, ready to take their orders. Karen selected the cheapest item on the menu, chili. Despite what Mitch said, she knew he didn't have much money. He had only been working a short time at the garage and most of his paycheck went into his car. She wasn't that hungry anyway, and the longer she sat there across from Chelsea, the less she felt like eating.

Dawn was still trying to make up her mind. "Maybe I'll live dangerously and have the lasagna. What do you think, Karen? Is it any good?"

"I wouldn't know," Karen snapped. What was the matter with Dawn? She knew Karen and Mitch had never eaten in this place before.

Dawn looked hurt and Karen regretted her harsh tone. Chelsea was leaning close to Ryan, speaking to him softly. Karen hated that. When Chelsea glanced over at her and Mitch, Karen was sure she had been talking about them. Yet she knew that however insensitive Chelsea could be at times, she had manners.

"How about that rain yesterday! Five inches!" Dawn said, in a brave attempt to bring everyone into the conversation. "I've never lived in a place where it rains that much. I'm not sure I like it."

"Too bad," Ian teased. "Hope you're handy with a snow shovel because we get tons of that, too. You won't see a blade of grass from Thanksgiving till Memorial Day. Last year we had eight feet on the ground before Christmas and —"

Just then Mitch accidentally knocked over his water glass. A cascade of ice cubes and water slid toward Chelsea. She jumped up, but not before a lapful splashed her miniskirt.

"I'm sorry —" Mitch began. "With all the flowers and stuff on the table —"

"Oh, no!" Chelsea dabbed at her sodden

skirt with a napkin. "Look at my skirt! It's soaked!"

Dawn handed Chelsea her napkin and said soothingly, "I'll go to the ladies' room with you. It's only water."

"But I'm drenched!" Chelsea cried, mopping her skirt dramatically.

Dawn looked as though she were about to cry. The whole evening was turning into a disaster. Mitch ran an exasperated hand through his brown hair. Karen knew how he hated scenes. There was only one thing for them to do.

She stood up and threw her linen napkin on the table, a flag of surrender. "I think Mitch and I ought to leave. We shouldn't have come."

"No, wait —" Dawn leaped to her feet. "We all just got off on the wrong foot."

"Sit down, you two," Ian urged. "Let's start over."

"I can't sit here in wet clothes," Chelsea complained. "I ought to go home and change." She tossed Mitch an annoyed look.

This isn't fair, Karen thought. It's my fault for dragging Mitch into this.

"Nice try," Ryan said to Dawn. "I told you it wouldn't work. Smoking the peace pipe was a good idea, but getting along with milltowners is asking too much."

Mitch was slow to get angry, but when he did, there was no telling what he might do. "I'd like to see how you and Miss Wonderful manage on our side of town. Take away your maids and waiters and fancy guards and you couldn't fight your way out of a wet paper bag."

Ryan's dark eyes glittered with challenge. "You calling me a snob?"

"If the stuffed shirt fits. . . ."

Ryan's answering smile was relaxed, in a dangerous sort of way. "Okay. I'm a sport. We'll do it your way, Boyd. Chels, want to go slumming?"

"I might as well. I'm too wet to go anywhere else." Karen recognized the keen edge of excitement in Chelsea's voice, despite the glum words. Chelsea Chrystal loved nothing better than the unexpected, a walk on the wild side.

"I thought you wanted to go home and change," Ryan said.

Chelsea waved him away, as if the spill never happened. "Don't be silly. It'll dry. Let's go!"

For her part, Karen was glad. She'd never come to this place again even if they whipped her with tire chains.

"We're leaving?" Dawn asked, dismayed to see the evening she had planned so carefully in tatters.

Ian, always genial, pushed his chair back with a scrape and said, "We're just moving the party to another location."

Outside in the parking lot, the three couples stood hesitantly, while Ian calculated the logistics of transporting six people. "My car's not big enough. What about yours, Mitch?"

"Forget it," Ryan broke in. "We'll take mine." He led them to a white Fifties Thunderbird parked under the lamplight. Karen knew a little about cars, enough to realize that this was a classic automobile.

"Where's your TR-7?" Ian asked Ryan, referring to the sportscar he usually roared around in.

"In the shop." Ryan unlocked the passenger door and gallantly helped Chelsea and Dawn into the backseat. One look at Karen's face and he merely said, "After you, madame."

The boys piled in the front seat and they took off, heading north. Ryan drove as fast as the law allowed and probably a little faster, Karen judged, sinking into blissfully rich leather upholstery. Beyond Rapid River, the trees thinned out and the familiar lights of businesses along Third Avenue illuminated the street in garish pinwheels.

Karen recognized the Handi-mart, Shroeder's Bakery, and the shoe repair shop with a sigh of relief. At last she was back in her own territory, where she belonged.

"Where to?" Ryan asked Mitch. "How about the bowling alley? Looks like there's action there."

Mitch pointed to Vincent's Diner, where a sputtering neon sign beckoned — or dared — hungry travelers to try the Chicken Fried Steak. "Pull in there. That is, if you can park this boat."

Chelsea leaned forward eagerly, her face

14

striped blue from the neon tubes outlining the doorway. "Is this a real diner? I've never been in a place like this before. I bet the jukebox has all Willie Nelson records."

A group of men stood by the front door, their faces gritty, as though they'd just received bad news.

Dawn said nervously, "Are you sure you want to eat here, Chelsea?"

"I know those men," Mitch said. "They work at the mill. With your dad, don't they, Karen?"

Karen climbed from the backseat. She recognized Gino Sabatini and Rudy Jenson, both on her father's shift. Their voices carried in the crisp November night.

"— bad time of the year to get sacked," Gino was saying. "With winter coming on."

"Leave it to the Chrystals to shut down half the mill right before Christmas," another man grumbled.

Karen exchanged a frightened glance with Mitch. Layoffs? At the mill?

"— necessary cutbacks, my foot," Rudy remarked, stomping on the stub of his cigarette which he dropped on snow-covered pavement. "Whenever Judge Chrystal gets in a bind, he takes it out on us. God knows when we'll get our jobs back. I guess I'll drift on up to Sunbury and see if my brother-in-law's got anything."

Karen couldn't believe what she was hearing. "Dad," she whispered to Mitch. "My father may be out of a job." She whirled on Chelsea. "Why didn't you tell me your family was laying off mill workers?"

Chelsea was genuinely astonished by the question. "I don't know anything about it, Karen. My father and grandfather don't discuss business with me."

"Why should they?" Karen accused. "It doesn't matter to you if people are out of work. Your daddy is a big-shot lawyer and your grandfather is a judge. *And* they own the mill. *You* won't suffer."

"I'm sorry, Karen. Really." Chelsea was close to tears. She wasn't used to being shouted at, and she was truly confused by Karen's attack. It wasn't *her* mill. What did Karen want from her?

Mitch put his arm around Karen protectively. "We'd better get home, Kar. They may need us."

Dawn stood by helplessly. The evening was over and it had been a total failure. Was there really any way for Karen and Chelsea, for Mill and Hill, to meet without explosions?

Chapter Two

On the end table, near the front door, there was a flat cedar box containing Bicycle playing cards. In tiny black letters, the words "Great Smoky Mountains, Tennessee" proclaimed that the cedar card box was a genuine souvenir from the Smokies, where Carl and Gloria Pickett spent their one-week honeymoon trip, before coming back to Chrystal Falls and settling down.

When Karen was little, she used to sit on the living room floor and open the cedar box, breathing in the mysterious, deepwood scents that still lingered. Mountains locked in the town of Chrystal Falls and a short drive in almost any direction would lead to woods as wild as anyone could want. But Karen's imagination, fired by the impressive words "Great Smoky Mountains," conjured pictures of primitive, almost prehistoric forests and majestic Indians stealthily tracking game through valleys scarfed in a bluish haze. What an exciting trip her parents must have had! And what a shame parents went on honeymoons before they had children — if only her parents had waited so she and Johnny could have gone, too.

Even at the age of six, Karen was planning to leave Chrystal Falls. She wanted to see new places, do important, wonderful things. She was determined not to grow up and become a mill worker's wife, yoked to a cramped, company-provided house, a budget that required eagle-eyed comparison shopping for the cheapest cuts of meat, and a lifetime of dreams as gossamer and untouchable as the haze that draped the Great Smoky Mountains.

Though she dreamed over the magical scent released by the cedar box, Karen also studied the intricate backs of the Bicycle playing cards within, running her finger along the mazelike design as though searching for a way out of milltown.

In first grade, the hardest lesson she had to learn wasn't mastering the alphabet in her blue-lined book, but discovering the vast difference between milltown children and those other children who lived on the Hill.

Karen would never forget walking down "A" Avenue with her brother Johnny on the first day of school. She swung her lunch box from one hand and walked with her head down, staring at her new patent-leather Mary Jane shoes, until Johnny, a big boy going into the third grade, told her to stop acting so stupid. When Karen looked up, she saw a yellow school bus driving down the street. The bus was empty and heading away from North Side Elementary.

"How come we don't get to ride that bus?" she asked her brother, who seemed to know everything. "How come we have to walk?"

"Because," Johnny said grudgingly, still aggravated that he had to escort his little sister to school, instead of walking with the guys. "North Side is only eight blocks from our house. All the kids walk. That bus goes to the other school."

"What other school?"

He sighed with great patience. "Chrystal Falls Elementary. That's where the rich kids go. You know, the kids that live in those fancy houses on the other side of town."

Karen had a vague idea of where he meant, but the concept of "rich" was still new to her. She was more concerned with keeping her new shoes from getting muddy. "How come we don't ride in *their* bus?"

"Because they think they're better than we are!" Johnny snapped. "And they won't ever let you forget it, either!"

From that day on, Karen equated "rich" with riding to school in a yellow bus that picked you up at your house. Sometimes she would sit in class, holding the fat pencil loosely in her fingers, her crooked letters forgotten for a moment, and dream about that other school, the one the rich kids went to. She imagined it had powder-puff carpeting and

19

vending machines that dispensed free candy bars and potato chips, and drinking fountains that ran with soda instead of plain water. The teachers pasted real gold stars on especially good papers, and there were clowns and magicians at recess.

She begged Johnny to tell her about the houses the rich kids lived in. When he said that he couldn't really see the houses, because they were enclosed with iron gates and surrounded by acres of woods and lawn, Karen envisioned towering castles in the sky. At the age of six, she had been dismayed to find out that not everyone lived in the rectangular, aluminum-sided boxes that marched in endless rows along streets bordering the mill. Things weren't equal, not one bit, and the older she got the more she resented it.

There was a different world beyond the mill, and beyond the fancy houses. She would leave milltown, she promised herself. She'd find that other world.

By the time Karen met Chelsea Chrystal in her freshman year at Chrystal Falls High, the chip on Karen's shoulder was stubbornly set. She knew that Chelsea lived in such a rarefied atmosphere that she and her friends never set foot in a vehicle as common as a school bus. They were chauffeured to school — and *their* shoes never got muddy. Learning that her childish idea of wealth was so far below reality only hardened Karen's attitude toward the kids on the Hill. Not that they cared. To Chelsea Chrystal and her friends, Karen and the other milltown kids were invisible. So why should Chelsea bother about such a trivial event as a layoff at the mill?

The disastrous triple date broke up in the parking lot of Vincent's Diner. Ryan drove them all back to the country club — he was stony silent at having his fun spoiled. Dawn, Chelsea, and Ian chattered about inconsequential events at school, desperately trying to pull the ragged edges of the evening together. But it was no use.

Mitch took Karen straight home. He was worried, too, she could tell. His father worked in another part of the mill than Karen's father, but rumors tended to fly around fast and furious when cutbacks occurred.

"It'll be okay," he told her when he parked in front of her house and shut off the headlights. "Those guys could've been blowing smoke."

"It didn't sound like smoke to me," Karen said. "Mitch, why have so many awful things happened this year? First the accident and you going to jail. Now my father's probably out of a job." She stared out of the car window at her house. The kitchen light was still on. Not a good sign. Usually her mother cleaned up after supper, then went in to watch TV with her father. The rest of the house was dark, and the unlit windows were like the gapped teeth of a jack o'lantern.

"We don't know that for sure," he said, leaning over to kiss her good-night. He tugged a lock of her hair and smiled. "I'll bet your dad's sitting in his favorite chair just like always, and you're out here worrying for nothing."

"I can't help it, Mitch. You heard those men."

He silenced the rest of her sentence with a soft kiss. "Did I tell you how pretty you look tonight? Is that a new sweater?"

He noticed! For the first time, Karen smiled. "Mitch, wasn't this evening just terrible?"

"Oh, I don't know. It isn't every day I get to dump a glass of water on Chelsea Chrystal." His grin became impish. "I kind of liked it."

Despite the horrible date, and Chelsea and Ryan, Mitch was still the wonderful guy Karen loved. She gave him another kiss — a longer, more tender one — to let him know she loved him and appreciated him.

"Give me a call if you need me," he said, opening her door.

"Thanks," Karen whispered, impulsively kissing him again. He was always understanding. Always there when she needed him.

When she let herself inside, the first thing Karen saw was the cedar card box lying on the floor by the front door. Her father's jacket lay across the end table where he had apparently thrown it, instead of hanging it over the back of his kitchen chair as he usually did.

The lid of the cedar box was broken and the Bicycle playing cards were strewn carelessly over the rug.

"For the eight hundredth time, the answer

is no," Carl Pickett said, looking up from the newspaper folded to the employment ads to glare at his wife. Four cigarette butts were drowned in the half-drunk cup of coffee at his elbow. He had quit smoking two years ago, but now he bought a pack every day when he picked up the morning newspaper.

"Carl," Gloria Pickett murmured. "It would only be for a little while. To help pay the bills. Just till we got on our feet again."

"No. You're not getting a job and that's final!" he bellowed. "What will people think? That Carl Pickett is a lazy bum who can't support his family anymore?"

"Nobody thinks that."

"They will, if you go off to work while I sit here and twiddle my thumbs!"

Karen slumped over her bran cereal, wishing that Johnny was there to talk to. Ordinarily her older brother was not much of an ally. For one thing, he was hardly ever around.

When Chelsea's older brother Monty, Johnny's best friend, was shipped off to a prestigious private school that fall, Johnny disappeared for weeks, much to Karen's and her mother's distress.

"What did you expect?" Carl Pickett had raged. "Monty isn't the bad influence. Even with that Chrystal kid shut away, Johnny can't straighten out. That boy is nothing but trouble."

For reasons no one could ever understand, Johnny Pickett hung around Chelsea Chrystal's wild brother, Monty. Johnny and Monty

23

had met when they were very young, going to different elementary schools. It was Monty Johnny was referring to on that day when Karen wanted to know why they couldn't ride the school bus, and Johnny had answered that the Hill kids thought they were better than anyone else. A superior two years older than Johnny, Monty had rubbed in the fact that his father and grandfather were rich and famous and that Johnny, a milltown kid, would never amount to anything. Johnny promptly gave Monty a black eye and from that day forward, they became friends, to the dismay of their families. Private schools had done nothing to tame Monty's wildness and when he and Johnny were together, the combination was as volatile as gasoline and a lit match. "Thick as thieves" described their strange friendship aptly.

Johnny returned shortly after the layoff, refusing to confess where he'd been all that time. Yet Karen was suspicious. Why had he come back at all, to face his father's wrath? Although he'd rather die than admit it, Karen believed Johnny was nearby the whole time, and when trouble struck at the mill, he came back, in case he was needed. Johnny wasn't as bad as he acted.

This morning he had left early on some mysterious errand. Ever since her father had been home, breakfast — and every other meal — had become a battlefield. At night, long after Karen had finished her homework and was in bed, she could hear her parents arguing.

Nothing like this had ever happened before. They always watched pennies, but at least her father brought home a regular paycheck, something they could count on, and her parents loved each other and their children.

Now that security had been cut off, Carl had applied for unemployment insurance, grumbling his distaste at having to take the money. Karen understood his bitterness, but what was wrong with her mother accepting a part-time job as a receptionist at Hair Today? Wouldn't that be better than losing the house or bickering over money from daybreak until dark?

Now her mother stood at the sink, tears filling her dark brown eyes. "We're a family, Carl. We help each other. Why won't you let me help you?"

"You give me all the help I need right here, fixing my meals, raising these kids. Being here for me. How can you do that if you're off some place making appointments for old ladies getting their hair dyed?" He left the table abruptly, pushing the paper away in disgust, but he kissed his wife's cheek as he passed her.

What a chauvinist, Karen thought incredulously. She never realized how tradition-bound her father was until then.

As if reading her mind, her mother said, "He didn't mean that the way it sounded, Karen. It's been so hard lately. . . ." Her voice trailed off as her glance was drawn involuntarily to the stack of unopened bills piled in the wicker basket on the counter.

Karen followed that glance and knew her mother was really worried about making ends meet.

Gathering her books for school, Karen slipped the newspaper her father had been reading inside her notebook. If Dad won't let Mom get a job, than I'll get one. I just can't sit back while we all struggle, she thought.

In homeroom, she circled ads for jobs she felt she could handle. After biology, she stopped Mitch in the hall and took all his change.

"It's for a good cause," she told him, then dashed to the pay phones near the cafeteria.

Appointments for interviews didn't exactly drop in her lap. No one seemed impressed by her eagerness, her willingness to do any job, no matter how grubby, at any price. Even though she lied and said she was eighteen, prospective employers sensed she was younger and promised to take her name and number, which Karen translated as, "Don't call us, we'll call you."

In desperation, Karen dialed the phone number of the last ad she had marked — waitress wanted, experience necessary. She had never worked as a waitress, but she'd learn.

To her surprise, the person on the other end sounded as desperate as Karen felt. Could she come down that afternoon? Could she start work tomorrow? Two waitresses had quit recently and the manager of the restaurant seemed frantic.

"Ummm, sure," Karen lied, when he asked

if she had previous experience. He didn't say "as a waitress." She *had* worked this past summer at the supermarket to earn money for school clothes. Surprisingly, he didn't ask for references; he was that harried about filling the position.

Just like that, on the telephone, he gave her the job.

"Where is this place?" Karen asked, hating herself for sounding so stupid. "I mean, which restaurant?"

Her mouth opened when he gave her the address and told her to report to the dining room of the Chrystal Falls Country Club. The very place Karen had vowed never to go into again, even if her life depended on it. Well, one should never say never.

She ran home to do her homework and report to the country club to fill out an application and pick up her uniform.

Karen could hear voices raised in argument from the street, yards away from her house.

"— hanging around Monty Chrystal has given you big ideas," Carl was shouting, when Karen opened the front door. He must have been yelling for some time because his face, naturally pale, was beet-red. "Just remember who's boss around here and it isn't you, John Pickett. I ought to —"

"Carl, he's only trying to help," Gloria interceded. "Don't be so hard on him."

"That's right, defend him," Carl said, transferring his anger to his wife. "You always do, no matter what your precious Johnny does. I don't want anyone in *my* family at the country club."

Karen put her books on the sofa and walked over to where her brother was slouched. His dark brown hair, so like their mother's, fell over his forehead and his long legs were stretched out before him in a pose of utter dejection. When his mouth wasn't twisted sullenly like this, Johnny was heartbreakingly handsome. He often reminded Karen of James Dean in *Rebel Without A Cause*, one of her favorite late-show movies.

"Don't tell me you're in trouble again," she said under her breath. "You just got home."

"So what else is new?" he groused. "Does anything ever change around this place?"

"What did you do this time?"

"Believe it or not, I got a job . . . at the country club. I'm parking cars." He shook his head, puzzled. "You'd think I'd robbed a bank or something the way Dad's carrying on. I thought a few extra bucks would help out around here. Guess I was wrong."

Karen's heart tumbled to her stomach. If her father was this livid over Johnny taking a job at the club, how would he react to her news? There was only one way to find out.

"Daddy," she said, lifting her chin as if to meet a blow. "I have something to tell you."

"What is it, Karen?" he replied. "Can't you see I'm upset over Johnny right now?"

"You're going to get a lot more upset, I'm afraid. I got a job today, too. I start tomorrow . . . as a waitress at the country club."

"Not you, too! First my son and now my little girl, my daughter, out working because her father isn't." Carl looked exactly as Karen had imagined Julius Caesar looked when he was stabbed by his two closest friends. Betrayed.

"Daddy, please, it's not like that at all," she hastened to explain. "I hate just sitting around when things are so —"

"You don't have to say another word." Her father's tone was suddenly tired, all his anger burned out. "Since you don't think I can provide for you anymore, then maybe I'll just leave."

Without another word, he grabbed his jacket and stalked out the front door.

Chapter Three

"Hi, my name is Karen and I'll be your waitress tonight. Can I get you something from the bar?" Karen's smile felt stretched at the corners. This waitress business was not what it was cracked up to be.

While Perky Palmer and another girl looked over the menu, Karen slipped her right foot from her shoe and rubbed her aching arch on the soft carpet. Her feet hurt so bad that amputation at the knees would have been welcome right about then.

"I'll have a Coke," the other girl said finally. Karen recognized her from school. Her name was Hollis and she was in Karen's P.E. class. Hollis kept her eyes on the menu, obviously embarrassed that the captain of her volleyball team now waited tables.

Perky had no such delicacy. "What do you recommend, Miss?" The "miss" was laced with a heavy tinge of sarcasm and cold blue eyes raked Karen's uniform.

What Karen wanted to suggest would have gotten her fired instantly, so she gritted her teeth and said mildly, "The orange fizz is pretty good, I hear."

"Well, I don't know. Sometimes these waitresses push things that aren't that great," Perky remarked to Hollis, as if Karen had suddenly turned into a potted plant. "You really can't trust their judgment." To Karen she said airily, "I'll have a Coke, too. Lots of ice." With a disdainful finger she wiped the spotless butcher block surface before her. "This table is filthy. Clean it."

Karen should have expected this from Perky Palmer. The acid-tongued blond girl prided herself on being Chelsea Chrystal's closest friend, though Chelsea didn't think so. Perky had none of the grace that Chelsea had. She never tried to be nice, unless she thought it would get her something. Chelsea accepted Perky's adoration, but she knew Perky was nasty.

It was bad enough for Karen to come back to the very place she'd said she'd never enter on pain of death — to work yet! — but putting up with Hill kids was almost too much. Karen ordered Cokes from the bar, one with extra ice, and leaned against the counter, wishing she were anywhere but the country club.

The Grill Room, where all the Hill kids congregated, really wasn't a bad place to work.

Karen's uniform consisted of a white blouse, a black snap-on bow tie, and a bright red carpenter's apron, with deep pockets to hold cocktail napkins, straws, her order book, a pen, and the tips she scooped off the tables. She provided black slacks and low-heeled shoes. Tonight, her first night on the job, she took care of eight tables, bringing food and drinks from the bar.

She quickly learned which dishes the cook wanted pushed, and to serve from left to right, but clearing the table nearly did her in. One of the waiters, a blond boy with dimples and a quick smile, showed her what she was doing wrong.

"Put the biggest on the bottom," Marc instructed Karen after she dropped three plates and a handful of flatware. "Like this." He stopped his own work to demonstrate the precise art of stacking dirty dishes in swift, efficient movements.

"Thanks." Karen was glad she was strong enough to carry the heavy china plates along one arm.

"Haven't I seen you before?" Marc asked. He stared at her critically. "Yeah. You were in here the other night — with Chelsea Chrystal and Ryan Simpson and some other kids. I waited on you."

Karen had hoped he wouldn't remember. "I wasn't exactly *with* Chelsea Chrystal. And I didn't stay long."

The unspoken words ". . . and now you

work here . . ." hung between them, but Marc was too nice to voice what he was thinking. Karen was grateful to have a friend. She had a feeling she would need one before the night was over.

And she was right. The two girls waiting for Cokes were typical of the kids she'd have to wait on. Hill kids. Snobbish brats, Karen thought, who had nothing better to do than hang around the country club. Being in a subservient position made Karen fair game. Girls she knew from school were uncomfortable with her. Boys made crude remarks, as if Karen herself was on the menu. Before the early dinner hour was half over, Karen was exhausted, fending off rude comments — and sometimes a hand or two — and forcing herself to be polite. But Perky's insolence wrecked the composure she'd worked so hard to attain.

I have to do this for Dad, she reminded herself, taking the tray of Cokes over to Hollis and Perky. Perky bristled with impatience, as though Karen had taken an interminable time to get their drinks.

When they finally left, Karen cleared the table behind her, sweeping the tip into her pocket. She had to admit Hill kids tipped well, she thought, carefully stacking the plates and glasses as Marc had taught her. That's one good thing I can say for them.

As she laid down fresh paper place mats, a new couple came forward to claim the table.

"Karen!" Dawn said. "What on earth are

you doing here?" She ignored the chair Ian MacFarland had pulled out for her, staring at Karen.

"What does it look like? I'm working." She handed them menus. She'd have to get used to waiting on kids she knew; it was inevitable. Dawn was okay, though. Sighing, Karen added, "Sorry, Dawn. I didn't mean to bite your head off. It's my first night and I'm really nervous."

"Then we'll make it easy on you," Ian said. "Two Cokes and two hamburgers — well done. The hamburgers, that is."

Dawn watched Karen scribble the order on her pad. "What's happening, Karen? I haven't seen you since . . . the other night. Is everything okay?"

"No, it's not. My father was laid off from the mill, at least until Christmas, maybe longer. That's the worst part, not knowing if he'll have a job when the layoff is over. Johnny's outside parking cars. Did you see him?"

Dawn shook her head.

"Well, there you have it," Karen said, smiling, pretending to joke. "The two poor Mill kids being good little soldiers, waiting on you rich kids to earn a few pennies."

"Wait a minute," Ian protested. "Just because we come here doesn't make us one of —"

"It's all right, Ian," Dawn said. "I understand how it is, Karen. When my father died, it was awful, not knowing where our next dollar was coming from."

Karen managed to smile genuinely for the first time that night. "I'll get your Cokes." Dawn was a tough person to figure. She and her brother lived on the fringes of the Hill. Dawn's mother was a doctor, as was Ian's father, so they weren't exactly living hand to mouth like the people in milltown. Yet Dawn didn't throw her status around, the way Perky did. Karen sensed a strange ambivalence about Dawn Newhouse — Dawn seemed to move between the Hill and Mill, refusing to take sides. She acted as friendly with Karen as she did with Chelsea.

Yet Karen felt that a fascination with milltown — and one milltown boy in particular — smoldered within Dawn, lurking just beneath the easygoing surface. Tonight that personality split was even more evident. Dawn clearly was not happy being there with Ian.

As she brought their hamburgers and fries, Karen overheard Ian say, "— or we could go to a movie. We didn't have to come here."

"You were hungry," Dawn answered, picking at the corner of her napkin. "And the Club was close. Besides, we went to the Inn Saturday and a movie Sunday night. I don't expect you to spend a fortune on me every night, Ian."

"What *do* you expect?" He gave Dawn an intense look.

Karen felt embarrassed as she set down their plates and offered them catsup.

Dawn seemed glad of the interruption. "Food's here! It looks great, Karen."

"I didn't do anything, Dawn. Just brought it out."

Dawn told Ian, "You ought to see Karen in Phys. Ed. She's a hundred places at once on the volleyball court. The only game I'm any good at is Crab Soccer."

"What's that?" Ian asked, biting into his hamburger.

"It's not really a game," Karen explained. "More like a free-for-all. Have you ever played volleyball on your back?"

"Can't say that I have." Ian slathered catsup on his french fries. "Am I about to hear some deep, dark, girl's-locker-room secret?"

Karen giggled. "Hardly. There are two teams, roughly, and we use a big, canvas beach ball —"

"And we have to lie down and hit the ball with our feet," Dawn finished. "If we want to move around, we lift up our butts and scuttle around on our hands and feet, like crabs. Everybody runs into everybody else. Doesn't that sound exciting?"

Ian wiggled his eyebrows lasciviously. "It sure does. Especially the running into each other part. I can't wait till your next game."

He said it lightly, but Dawn didn't laugh. Instead, she looked down at her plate and bit her lip.

The dinner hour picked up and Karen was busier than ever. She passed Dawn's and Ian's table several times in the course of the evening, noting little conversation between them. The few times they did speak, words were exchanged tersely. Karen thought Ian was a nice guy, but Dawn behaved as though she wanted him to vanish.

Someone was distracting Dawn to the point of losing Ian. And if that someone was Pete Carter, as Karen suspected, trouble was brewing for Dawn.

The rest of the night was blurred by a collage of sounds: barked orders for food, blaring music, the clatter of dishes, and spikes of laughter that punctured the drone of a roomful of kids, all talking at once.

Karen was so glad when her shift was over, she nearly sat down on the floor and cried.

Marc patted her shoulder. "There, the worst is over. You lived. And tomorrow night you can come in and do it again."

"I'm not so sure," she groaned. "My feet!"

"I have the perfect cure for sore feet."

"Not dancing, I hope."

"Whenever the old dogs start moanin', just think about your tips. Works every time."

He had a point. Her salary wasn't that great — just minimum wage — but her tips could be substantial if she worked hard. As she got used to the work, she could take on more stations. Her feet throbbed at that cheery prospect.

When Mitch picked her up at the front gate, Karen hurled herself in the front seat like a sack of potatoes.

"Hello to you, too," Mitch said. "Is this the thanks I get, driving all the way up here after a tough evening at the garage?" He leaned over and kissed her.

"Your evening couldn't possibly be worse than mine. If I never see another slice of pizza, it'll be too soon."

"And just what I had a craving for!" he teased. "Seriously, Karen, it's not that late. Want to do something?"

"Just so long as it doesn't require standing or walking. My feet have checked out for the night."

"It wasn't your feet I had in mind." Spinning the wheel, Mitch turned the car toward the secluded overlook by the river that had become their special stopping-place.

Killing the engine, he leaned over to take Karen in his arms. Karen submitted to his kiss, but couldn't respond. When she felt Mitch stiffen, she knew he was angry.

"What's with you?" he said, pulling back.

"I'm tired. I just worked five hours on my feet, being polite to Chelsea's friends and taking guff from Perky Palmer."

"So that's it." Mitch drummed his fingers on the dash. "You knew when you took the job it would be this way, Karen."

"That doesn't make it any easier."

"So quit. Call up your boss tomorrow and tell him you quit. Takes ten seconds. You told me your father hit the roof when you got the job in the first place."

"He did. It was bad enough that Johnny got work at the country club, but when I did, too — well, Dad practically crumbled. He's so proud, Mitch. He can't stand the thought that he isn't supporting his family. And it's not his fault — jobs are scarce since the layoff."

"Jobs were scarce long before the layoff," Mitch said wryly. "I mean it, Karen. You really ought to quit."

"I can't do that, Mitch! Have you forgotten *my* father got laid off?" This was a sore spot between them — Mitch's father was not among the employees caught by the temporary cutback.

"My dad's been laid off before," Mitch said defensively.

"Then you know what it's like. When the mill whistle blows shift changes, Dad jumps up like he's going to work . . . and then he remembers and it's like he's been fired all over again."

"But he didn't *lose* his job."

"How do you know?" Karen accused, suddenly angry at Mitch's complacent attitude. "How do you know what those Chrystals will do next? They don't care about us! Nobody cares whether we live or die down here."

"Stop overreacting. See what this job is doing to you?"

"It's not the job — it's this town!" She realized then what Mitch was driving at. "You don't think I can handle working, do you?"

"I didn't say that."

"You never say much of anything, that's your trouble."

Karen knew she was being rotten. Mitch was so wonderful and always there when she needed him. But he lacked . . . fire. That was it. Mitch seldom got steamed up over the injustices that were everyday occurrences in milltown, preferring the ostrich approach of sticking his head in the sand until the worst blew over.

But what was even more unforgivable, in Karen's mind, was his lack of ambition. Mitch fully expected to go to work in the mill someday, just like his father and his grandfather before him.

"Don't you want *more*?" Karen asked him once. "How can you settle for this?"

"It was good enough for my father . . ." was Mitch's stock answer.

Karen couldn't believe anyone would willingly stay in milltown. She tried tempting Mitch with stories of exotic places she'd like to visit, exciting things she planned to do, but he'd say mildly, "That's nice, Karen," as if humoring a two-year-old. "If you're lucky, you'll see all those places."

Karen wasn't about to entrust her future to something as capricious as luck. She intended to forge her own destiny, even if it meant waiting on Chelsea Chrystal and Perky Palmer every night for the next ten years.

I'll keep that job, she resolved, sore feet and all.

One driving thought would get her through this whole ordeal: someday she would leave Chrystal Falls and she'd never look back.

But when Mitch took her home that night, leaning over to kiss her good-night as if no

40

harsh words had ever passed between them, Karen began to have doubts. Was working at the club worth the blisters on her heels, worth the added tension in her house? Worth fighting with Mitch about?

Looking at him now she saw love and admiration shining from his sweet brown eyes. No matter what, she couldn't lose Mitch. What he lacked in fiery ambition, he more than made up for in steadfastness. Mitch would go to the ends of the earth for her, on his knees, if he had to.

Karen threw her arms around him and hugged him as if she'd never let him go.

"What's that for?" he asked, surprised.

"For putting up with me."

He was smiling when she got out of the car and suddenly her feet didn't hurt quite so much. Besides, she had enough ambition for two.

Chapter Four

Dawn was having a hard time concentrating. Ordinarily she gave English, her favorite subject, full attention, but today the poems of Edgar Lee Masters didn't interest her in the least.

For one thing, Mr. Elkins, who was reading several selections from *The Spoon River Anthology* in his strident, slightly sarcastic voice, totally shattered the sensitivity in Masters' poems about the inhabitants of a small town, as revealed through their epitaphs.

The man should definitely find another line of work, Dawn decided, tuning him out.

But she couldn't blame the English teacher entirely for her wandering thoughts. It was the argument with Ian last night. Or rather, the argument she *didn't* have.

Dawn sighed, putting her head down on her notebook. It should have been a perfectly wonderful date. But somewhere between the how-are-you and the hamburgers, the evening soured.

Ian had taken her out almost every day for two weeks, even if they only drove around and got a Coke. Dawn liked Ian, she really did. His golden-brown eyes had captured her interest from the first moment she saw him standing in the hallway of her Uncle Walt's house. And he had eased those first bumpy days at school, introducing her to his friends, showing her around, throwing her a lifeline when she feared she might drown in a sea of conflicting viewpoints and confusing situations. Chrystal Falls presented a puzzle she didn't think she'd solve in a million years. Ian provided a cushion of sanity. More important, he was there to pick up the pieces when Pete Carter broke off with her.

Silently, Dawn ticked off Ian's virtues. He was handsome, well-mannered, but not so stuffy that he didn't know how to have a good time, and smart. He made her feel as though she was the only girl in the entire world, when they were together. But he was too bland, too predictable. He was vanilla ice cream and Oreo cookies — comfortable, familiar, a kindergarten snack.

I should be shot at sunrise, Dawn scolded herself. Here I have a terrific boy at my feet and I'm going to throw him away.

She didn't want vanilla ice cream. She wanted Rocky Road — a jumble of textures and flavors that made her crave scoop after scoop.

She wanted Pete Carter.

Last night's date only served to point out to her she was with the wrong boy. It wasn't Ian's fault. He behaved impeccably, as usual, asking her what she wanted to do, where she wanted to go, what she wanted to eat. After five minutes or so of this, Dawn longed to scream, "Do what *you* want for a change!" Ian finally admitted he was hungry and when he suggested going to the country club, Dawn sighed with relief. At last, he'd asserted himself.

When they were seated at their table, Dawn was stunned to find Karen Pickett working as a waitress. Ian tried to make light of the situation by putting both her and Karen at ease, but Dawn still felt engulfed by guilt. The triple date she'd arranged between Karen and Mitch and Chelsea and Ryan, a futile attempt to bridge the galaxy-wide chasm between Hill and Mill, had backfired. And the layoffs had made things much worse.

Dawn saw the barricade between Karen and Chelsea rise higher. It represented a century of mistrust, betrayal, and resentment. As long as Chelsea's family held the purse-strings of Karen's family, through ownership of the mill, the barrier was insurmountable.

But she didn't have to play by those rules. And she *wouldn't*. If she spent the rest of her days in Chrystal Falls, she wouldn't knuckle under to the prejudice the others accepted as the normal course of life here.

Brought back to the present by Karen bringing their sandwiches, Dawn asked Ian, "Don't you ever want to do something wild and crazy?"

"Like what?"

"I don't know." Did she have to supply his answers now? "Something a little risky."

He bit a french fry in half with mock ferocity. "Well, once in a while, when I'm feeling really courageous, I eat lunch in the school cafeteria. How's that for danger?"

"You know what I mean."

He assessed her tone and replied evenly, "If you mean, do I ever have a yen to jump from a plane or play chicken with an oncoming train, the answer is no."

"That's not what I meant," Dawn said, frustrated. "I just wondered if you get bored doing the same old thing, day after day."

"Of course I get bored. Who doesn't? I get up every morning, go to school, have a little fun in between if I can, and go to bed every night. It's called living. But just because I get bored, doesn't mean I'm going to knock over a Handi-Mart for a quick thrill." He put down his hamburger to stare at her. "What's with you tonight, Dawn? You're acting weird."

She *felt* weird, as though she were caught in a time-warp, trapped in a crack between the second and third dimensions. She should have been telling Ian funny stories about school, not interrogating him, trying to make him confess some quirk in his character. They should have been laughing like the other couples in the dining room. Instead, they ate

45

their sandwiches in an uncomfortable silence.

He drove her home, wrapped in that same thick silence. With one hand on the car door, Dawn attempted to redeem the miserable evening.

"Thanks for dinner, Ian. Will I see you after school tomorrow?"

"I doubt it. I'm going to be pretty busy." He stared straight ahead. In the bright lamplight of the apartment parking lot, she saw his grimly-set jaw.

"Well," she faltered, "at least you'll be in history class. What about lunch afterward?" She wanted to let him know she liked him, that she wasn't a thoughtless clod.

"Don't count on it." He turned the key in the ignition. "I think I'll have to recover from dinner first."

As she undressed in her bedroom, Dawn knew who had ruined her date with Ian. Someone miles away from the country club. Someone who didn't care the least that she had given up the nicest boy in the world for him. Someone who had thrown her love back in her face when she offered it to him.

Pete Carter.

Now Dawn raised her head from her notebook. He was there — sitting three seats behind her. He had come into class seconds after the late bell, giving Mr. Elkins an insolent nod that should have been grounds for a trip to the office. Then he'd brushed past Dawn to take the only available seat.

His presence filled the classroom, or at least it seemed that way to Dawn. And his presence filled her mind, too. When she looked down at her notebook, she was astonished to see Pete Carter's name scribbled along the margins of her half-finished English notes.

What's the matter with me? she berated herself. I'm regressing into my second childhood.

Next, she'd be playing that old game where she wrote a boy's name over hers and crossed out common letters, then chanted "love, hate, friendship, marriage" with the remaining letters, to predict their future.

She quickly closed her notebook before anyone could see the incriminating doodles, sat up alertly, and tried to pay attention to the teacher.

Don't think about Pete's long legs, she instructed herself. Forget about his dark eyes. . . .

It was no use. She kept remembering those hours they had spent together — walking the dog down by the river, having snacks in a coffee shop. Not really dates, more like slices of time carved from the everyday world.

Having sufficiently mangled "Emerson Rush," Mr. Elkins began to recite "Robert Chapin," one of the poems Dawn liked best. She winced in anticipation.

" 'Have you stood in front of the iron bars, And watched the lion look over your head? He sees the palm-tree and the —' "

* * *

A piercing *beep-beep* suddenly blasted from the P.A. system. Everyone sat frozen for a few seconds, as the message penetrated. A fire drill? Or the real thing?

"All right, get moving," Mr. Elkins commanded. "You know what to do."

Maybe the rest of his students knew what to do, but Dawn didn't. She had missed fire drill procedure, starting a few days late. Either that or Chrystal Falls babies were briefed at birth on what to do during a high school fire drill. The class swirled around her as she stood by her desk in confusion.

A hand clutched her elbow. It was Pete. "This way, Newhouse."

In the hall, the progression to the nearest exit was mostly orderly, if ear-splitting. The fire alarm continued to squawk and kids were yelling at each other. Pete firmly steered Dawn through the door, shielding her body from a senior football player who evidently didn't even see her. He led her to the parking lot where she recognized Perky and a few others from English.

It was cold outside, and Dawn's L. L. Bean jacket was in her locker. But the chills that rippled across her shoulders weren't entirely due to the temperature. Pete Carter hadn't spoken to her for weeks — not since that dreadful day at the river when he declared everything was off between them — and here he was standing close to her. So close.

"Thanks," she told him, somewhat stiffly.

"I'd probably still be in there, if you hadn't showed me out."

"Elkins should have looked out for you. He knows you're new. But let's face it, the man has a mental deficiency."

She didn't know what to say to that, so she changed the subject. "Think it'll burn down?" she said, looking at the school.

"No such luck."

It seemed strange, carrying on a conversation with him, even swapping remarks as innocuous as these. How could he stand next to her and not remember their parting at the river? She could still hear his last words ringing in her ears and would until the day she died. "Good-bye, Newhouse. For keeps."

He noticed her shivering. "You're cold, aren't you?" Without another word, he took off his leather jacket and draped it over her shoulders. If he were anyone else, it would have been a gallant gesture, a boy-girl thing that Dawn could have interpreted as a definite sign. But with Pete, she wasn't sure.

"Thanks," she said weakly. "But won't you get cold?"

"I was too hot with that coat on, anyway."

Is that a fact? she thought. Perhaps he wasn't as cool as he appeared.

"Do they have these drills often?" she asked. "At my other school, they'd give us a day's warning, so we could keep our coats with us."

"Are you kidding? You better pray this is only a fire drill and not a bomb scare."

"Bomb scare?" Dawn had visions of S.W.A.T. teams storming the halls, with barking dogs trained to sniff out bombs.

He nodded. "Last year, we had one every five minutes, practically. And always at the same time. During my lunch shift. And the cops took forever, checking all the lockers. After five or six scares, I just took my tray out to the parking lot. I got tired of missing lunch every day. Now if they have those things during class time, that's okay."

Dawn wondered about Pete's contemptuous attitude toward school. He never carried a notebook or textbooks, but whenever he was called on in English or history, he always gave clear, concise answers. Undermotivated, that's what her mother would say. Bright but bored. Or troubled.

She was reminded of the poem Mr. Elkins was in the process of slaughtering when the fire drill buzzer sounded. "Life is a cage! Beauty a vision of freedom once enjoyed." Pete was a lot like that lion, staring out of his cage.

She wished she could take his hand, feel his warm fingers curl over hers, stroke the fine black hairs on the back of his arm. Give me the green light, she pleaded silently. I'll meet you halfway. More than halfway. Come to me!

"You and MacFarland seem pretty tight," he said with exaggerated nonchalance. "You going with him?"

"No. We're just — friends." If Ian heard her say that, he'd be mortified. Irrationally, she didn't want Pete to think she was pining away for him, even though it was true. "What's it to you if I am going with him?"

"Just wondering."

"His father and my mother work together at the hospital. Ian was the first person I met when I came to town." And you were the first to break my heart. "Naturally we'd be friends."

"Naturally you'd be friends with those people," Pete corrected, almost angrily.

"What's that supposed to mean?"

"Just what I said. You spend a lot of time up on the Hill, I notice."

"Not all. I go down to the river almost every night with Abner." You couldn't throw out a bigger hint than that.

"Do you? Well, maybe I'll see you there one of these nights." It was almost a dare.

"Maybe you will." Dawn forced herself to sound equally casual. Ian would be hurt if he found out she saw Pete Carter. But her desire for him was too strong.

"And maybe," he paused, "maybe we'll go have a bite at Mom and Pops." So he hadn't forgotten the good times they'd had at the little restaurant he used to take her to.

The cold lump in her stomach suddenly thawed. "Sounds good."

He laughed that wonderful rich laugh and then the "all clear" bell rang. Students began moving reluctantly toward the school.

Somehow Dawn got separated from Pete. "Your jacket!" she called.

"Keep it," he yelled back, and then was swept away in the tide of kids surging through the doorway.

A smile tugged at her lips. She knew why he let her keep his coat — to have a reason to call her. Life was suddenly looking up!

Perky Palmer passed her with a knowing smirk. Undoubtedly, she had seen Dawn and Pete talking. So what? Nothing was going to ruin Dawn's joy.

When Dawn spotted the tall, slender blond girl ahead of her, she wanted to express her exuberance.

"Hey, Chelsea! How's it going?"

Chelsea Chrystal turned around to see who was calling her, her expression distant. "Oh, Dawn. Hi."

"See you after school today?" Dawn asked. "Chels, did you hear me?"

But Chelsea had walked away from her, heading toward the girls' room without even telling Dawn good-bye.

What's wrong with her? Dawn thought.

Plenty was wrong with Chelsea. She had received the strangest phone calls the night before.

She had just stepped from the shower, her head turbaned in a towel, her body swathed in a fluffy bath sheet, when the phone had rung. Maybe it's Josh, she'd hoped, though Dawn's handsome older brother had no reason to call her. Still, Chelsea believed if she wished for something hard enough, it would come true. And she was attracted to Josh.

Be Josh, be Josh, she willed as she picked up the receiver.

"Is this Chelsea Chrystal?" the muffled voice asked. It was a guy, but definitely not Josh Newhouse.

"Yes, it is."

"Just checking." Then the man hung up.

Chelsea sat down on her bed and stared at the phone, puzzled. Then she shrugged and began drying her short, damp hair. The phone rang again. If this is somebody's idea of a joke, she thought, it's not very funny.

She jerked the receiver from its cradle and said "Hello." There was silence. She blurted, "Whoever you are, stop pestering me!" She waited.

Laughter poured smoothly into her ear.

"Who is this?" she demanded.

"Next time, baby." He hung up with a soft click.

Who was that guy? How did he get her unlisted number? And what did he want?

Chapter Five

"I'm putting you in the main dining room tonight," Karen's boss told her when she reported to work one evening. "Estelle called in sick. You're about her size. I think she keeps an extra uniform in the closet. Hurry up, I need to brief you on the menu."

The main dining room! Karen's stomach lurched. It was one thing to wear a red carpenter's apron and serve hot dogs and pizza to kids in the Grill Room. But to wait on Chrystal Falls' movers and shakers who patronized the Valley Forge Room was quite another matter.

But she couldn't argue. She had taken this job under false pretenses — her boss believed she had experience — so she had no one to blame except herself.

In the lounge reserved for the help, Karen found the extra red satin blouse and short black skirt the manager had mentioned. As she cinched the gold fringed sash around her small waist, Karen immediately hated what she saw in the full-length mirror: The red blouse was cut too low and the short skirt made her feel more like an imposter than ever — a girl masquerading as a grown woman, an inexperienced kid pretending to be a real waitress. She made a face at her reflection, then went out to brave the ogres in the dining room.

In the Valley Forge Room, decorated in a patriotic theme with lots of red, white, and blue, Karen was instructed to fill the teak salt and pepper mills and to fold the heavy blue damask napkins into a tricky design called Bishop's Mitre, then place the napkins on each gold-rimmed place setting on the red-skirted tables. She suspected the other waitresses were making the most of Estelle's last-minute replacement.

Before the dinner hour went into full swing, Karen had to memorize the specials of the evening — soup, fish, poultry, and beef dishes, and two desserts — which all had French names impossible to pronounce, much less memorize.

The captain led a well-dressed older couple to one of Karen's stations and suddenly she was paralyzed with fear, forgetting everything she was supposed to do. Her feet, tap-dance light on the volleyball court, felt as though twenty-pound barbells were strapped to them. The captain crooked a warning finger at her, galvanizing her into action.

"My name is Karen and I'll be your waitress for this evening. May I take your drink order while you look over the menu?" she said in the modulated voice she adapted to suit the luxurious surroundings. Because she was under twenty-one, she was not allowed to serve drinks, only take the order to the bartender.

The gentleman consulted his companion, then asked for a bottle of wine, giving the year and French name so fast Karen had to make him repeat it twice before she got it straight.

Mitch was right, she thought. I *don't* belong here.

When she brought salads to the table with the wrong dressings, she knew she'd never get through this night. And when the gentleman fussily asked for a chilled salad fork, scorning the room-temperature salad fork Karen pointed out, she decided she really didn't care whether she made it through the night or not.

Karen looked up to see Chelsea Chrystal lounging in the arched doorway, like a very rare and expensive plant that needed watering, and casting a quick glance around the room. When she was certain every eye was glued to her, she flashed a smile calculated to melt the bartender's ice cubes, then glided up to the captain's desk, who, to Karen's disgust, nearly groveled at Chelsea's feet, welcoming her effusively.

Perky Palmer, two boys Karen didn't know, and Chelsea's little sister Amy followed in

Chelsea's wake. They were led to the best table in the room, one conspicuously empty all evening, and located in the middle of the dining room where everyone could see them and where they, like kings and queens presiding over a royal banquet, could observe the room.

Unfortunately for Karen, this was also her station.

Not them, Karen groaned inwardly. Anybody but them.

The two boys held out chairs for the girls. Chelsea rewarded her escort with another high-voltage smile that could have lit the entire town during power failure. Even if she hadn't smiled, her dazzling outfit packed enough kilowatts to illuminate a football field.

Tonight she wore a silver dress that swirled just above her knees. Sparkling arrows climbed the length of her shimmery hose, and the three-inch chrome-colored sandals encasing her slim feet made the rest of the shoes in that room look like rubber boots. Tiny crystal triangles hung from her earlobes, setting off her short haircut, declaring to the world she was the one and only Chelsea Chrystal.

By comparison, Perky looked dull in a pink silk chemise that was cut even lower than Karen's blouse. Her waist-length golden hair was caught high in a rhinestone clasp, then allowed to fall over one shoulder. Like her clothes, Perky's hair was too perfect, too "done." With her short, layered cut, Chelsea was able to carry off her glamorous outfit with exactly the right touch of irreverence.

Chelsea's sister Amy looked adorable in a green velvet jumper with a red ribbon in her hair.

Karen couldn't put it off any longer. She had to wait on that table, much as she hated it. Pasting on a cardboard-stiff smile, she passed around the little gold-tasseled menus and greeted Chelsea and Perky as if they were like any other patrons she'd served that evening. From the look Perky gave her, Karen knew instinctively she was going to make her life miserable.

Give me strength, she prayed.

Perky started. "I thought if we ate in here, we'd avoid the help from the Grill Room." She addressed the table, but Karen knew full well the remark was directed at her.

"The room we passed?" the dark-haired boy asked. "Didn't you say you practically lived in that place?"

"I do," Perky added hastily. "The food's great, but the service. . . ." She rolled her eyes skyward as her hand described a "so-so" motion. "Daddy told me to take you and Richard someplace especially nice. I hope we won't be disappointed. Some of these new waitresses look terribly inefficient, don't you think so, Richard?"

"I wouldn't say that," the boy sitting next to Chelsea replied. "She looks okay to me. More than okay." He gave Karen a big wink and it was all she could do to keep from decking him.

Perky shook a red-nailed forefinger at her water goblet, indicating that Karen should have filled the glasses by now.

Amy smiled when Karen filled her glass. "Hi, Karen. How are you?"

"Fine, thank you." Karen had to admit that Amy was decent. But then, she was just a kid. Give her time.

Amy chattered on while Karen poured water into the goblets, as though Karen were a guest at their table instead of their waitress. "I didn't know you were working here. Do you like it? I bet you get to eat all the leftover desserts, don't you? Have you met Perky's cousins? This is James and this is Richard. They live in Philadelphia, only they're visiting here —"

"Amy, for heaven's sake," Perky rebuked her harshly. "Will you be quiet? Why did you have to bring her along, anyway?" she added to Chelsea.

"I told you once. No one was going to be home tonight. Not even the help. And don't talk to her that way, Perky. Amy's a love." Chelsea's tone was light, but Perky knew she was irritated, and Chelsea Chrystal was not one to be crossed.

Karen had other patrons to serve. She rattled off the specials of the evening, then left to bring out the basket of hot homemade bread. Colonial foods were the pride of the Valley Forge Room.

As Karen set down individual saucers of molded butter pats, Chelsea asked, trying to be friendly, "Why are you working in here, Karen? Did you get promoted from the Grill?"

"I'm subbing for the regular waitress who called in sick," she answered, wishing they would give her their orders so she could get away.

But Perky's cousins were still deliberating over the menu.

"I'll bet anything Karen does such a fantastic job here tonight that she'll be offered a promotion. The next thing you know, she'll be manager. Pretty soon she'll own the place." Perky laughed, an ugly sound.

"Ignore Perky," Chelsea advised Karen. "She's had to entertain these two hunks the past week and she's a little off the wall."

Karen could see her point — Perky was always on stage whenever a good-looking boy was always so hostile to Chelsea. Was that a Chelsea was speaking to her in this half-confidential, half-joking tone, when Karen was always so hostile to Chelsea. Was that a Chrystal rule? Treat the help with respect?

The boys were also puzzled by so much attention being paid to the waitress. "Do you guys know each other?" James asked Chelsea.

"Karen goes to our school," Chelsea replied. Then she became businesslike. She ordered briskly, asking that her flounder be broiled in butter with *very* little lemon, her salad dressing on the side, not mixed, she wanted iced tea unsweetened, with lime slices, and an extra glass of ice.

Perky also gave a complicated order, pleased to see Karen scribbling furiously to get it all down. Her cousins and Amy ordered like normal people.

When she carried the order back to the kitchen, the manager grabbed her elbow. "How are we doing tonight, Pickett?" he asked, but she could see he clearly wasn't interested in their mutual welfare.

"Fine."

"Miss Chrystal and Miss Palmer getting all the attention they need?"

More than they deserve, Karen bit back. She nodded dutifully.

"Good. We don't want to make them unhappy, now do we? The Chrystals and the Palmers receive red-carpet treatment or we'll hear about it."

I'm sure *we* will, Karen thought acidly, knowing she'd be the one to pay if customers went away dissatisfied.

Her boss's warning didn't come a minute too soon. When the main courses were ready, Karen carried the heavy tray to the center table.

"The plate is hot, so please be careful," Karen cautioned, setting the platter before Chelsea.

"The plate may be hot, but this fish certainly isn't." Chelsea poked at it with her fork as though it were frozen solid. "Please take it back and have the chef fix me another piece."

"Certainly." Karen whisked away the offending flounder, nearly burning her fingers on the hot plate. The only cold fish in here, she consoled herself, resisting the reflex to suck her scorched hand, is not on this platter.

Instinctively, Karen knew Chelsea wasn't being nasty, that she just expected everything to be the way she wanted it. But it still made Karen angry.

When Karen brought out Chelsea's freshly-cooked fish, Chelsea smiled and said, "Thank you. It looks delicious."

But then Perky complained that her chicken was overdone and the rice was sticky. Karen was completely off-balance, her confidence destroyed. She ran back and forth, fetching a forgotten Coke, bringing hot tea instead of iced tea, dropping a biscuit on the floor.

The manager was furious. "What's the matter with you, Pickett? The center table looks like a Keystone Cops movie! Have you gone crazy? I specifically told you to roll out the red carpet for those people, not insult them!"

"I'm sorry, but it's not my fault. They keep changing orders and whatever I bring out isn't right." Karen fought back tears.

"Well, whose fault is it? The chef isn't a mind reader. He only prepares what you tell him! I'm going over there to apologize for you," he said, jerking at the knot of his tie. "But mark my words, Pickett, if I can't repair the damage and they walk out of here mad, you're in big trouble."

From the kitchen door, Karen watched as he bent over Chelsea and Perky, smiling too much.

"I promised them dessert on the house," he told Karen when he returned, "to make up for your bumbling. See if you can do that right!"

Perky's cousins were telling jokes when Karen served the chocolate cheesecake, wedges too large for any one person to eat. Perky ignored Karen completely, looking past her as she carefully set the plates before them, as if she was obstructing their view. Chelsea was uncomfortable and wished they had never come. Karen was not her enemy, even though she knew she was Karen's.

When they left, the table looked like a war zone. Napkins fluttered from chair seats, uneaten pieces of cheesecake lay on the plates. The pepper mill was overturned in a gritty spill. Perky had apparently cleaned out the contents of her purse, leaving a litter of chewing gum wrappers, wadded-up Hersey's Kisses foils, and lipstick-blotted tissues.

The dinner hour rush was over, to Karen's immense relief. The dining room was mostly empty. Only a few people lingered over coffee. The conversation, so bright and animated earlier, had dimmed. Karen could hear the captain usher in a couple behind her as she picked up plates from the center table. He seated the new people at one of her stations. Would this night ever end?

"Enjoy your meal, Mr. Chrystal, Mrs. Chrystal," the captain said. "Your waitress will be right with you."

That's me, Karen thought without enthusiasm. More Chrystals. Just what I need.

She half-turned so she could maneuver the dirty plates onto her tray in one movement, as she'd learned. From the corner of her eye, she saw a man — so faultlessly groomed he could have doubled for a department-store mannequin — help a woman slip out of her fur coat.

Too young to be Judge Chrystal, Karen determined. He must be Alexander Chrystal, Chelsea's father. And the woman was her mother Elizabeth. How lucky could she get? Bring on the whole family!

At that same moment, the man caught sight of Karen.

"Gloria," he breathed. "Gloria?" he said again, a little uncertainly.

Karen stared at him. Gloria? He had said her mother's name!

"What did you say, Alex?" Elizabeth turned to her husband, her beautiful face frowning.

"Nothing, my dear," he soothed his wife, but his blue eyes were still locked on Karen, his expression incredulous.

Karen didn't know what to do. Chelsea's father kept staring at her, his flawless composure frankly disturbed.

"Can I help you?" Karen managed at last,

her voice shaky under Alexander's unnerving gaze.

"I — I'm sorry. For a moment I thought you were Glo — a girl I once knew."

"Alex, for heaven's sake, why are you badgering this poor girl?" Elizabeth's words were meant to be sympathetic, a little amused, but the eyes she turned on Karen said otherwise. She did not appreciate her husband stammering and gazing awestruck at a young waitress.

"I'm terribly sorry, miss," he addressed Karen, once more the suave man who first walked into the restaurant. "I didn't mean to startle you. But you reminded me of someone I knew a long time ago. Please accept my apology."

Karen said nothing. There'd been no mistaking the tone in his voice when he whispered her mother's name. It was tender, joyful. The voice of someone who had lost someone he loved . . . and suddenly found her again.

Chapter
Six

Her mother was still up when Karen got home, sitting in the living room, a book face down over one knee. "You're late tonight, Karen," she said. "Did you and Mitch go somewhere before he brought you home? I don't like you staying out on school nights."

Karen shook her head. "We didn't go anyplace. I'm late because I had to work in the main dining room tonight and it took me longer to finish up." She decided to omit the tongue-lashing she'd received from her boss about the Great Center Table Fiasco.

"Oh, really?" Gloria Pickett closed her book and laid it on the end table. "A promotion, Karen? Are you going to be working there from now on? That's exciting."

Not half as exciting as what happened when Alexander Chrystal walked in, Karen thought. But aloud she said, "It's not what you think,

Mom. It was only for one night. A last-minute replacement, that's all."

She made a big show of unwinding her wool scarf and tucking her gloves in the deep pocket of her stadium coat to avoid her mother's face. She wanted to ask her mother about Chelsea's father, but how? Blurt out, "Mr. Chrystal saw me tonight only he thought it was you and he sounded like a long-lost lover, what do you think of that?"

Maybe it wasn't anything. Alexander Chrystal and her mother seemed about the same age — they'd probably known each other for years. But Karen couldn't remember her mother ever mentioning Chelsea's father. And there had been plenty of opportunities. Ever since Johnny started hanging around with Monty Chrystal, the subject of the Chrystal family had come up more than a few times.

"You're tired tonight, aren't you?" Gloria observed with a cluck of concern. She rose to go into the kitchen. "How about some hot chocolate? Change into your pajamas and robe and come on out when you're ready. Okay?"

Karen gave her a weak smile. Jammies and robe. She hadn't worn pajamas since she'd gotten too big for her Dr. Denton's. Mothers never seem to notice their children are growing up, she said to herself. Even though this particular child had been working in an adult role the whole night and learned with a shock that her mother might have had another life, long ago.

In her room, Karen switched on the light, waking Horatio who uncurled and stretched from his nest on her pillow, blinking stupidly.

"Thanks loads, cat," Karen said. "You know how I love to sleep with fuzzy cat hairs up my nose. Good thing I'm not allergic." Actually, she adored Horatio and would have let him sleep on her stomach the entire night if he wanted, all thirteen pounds of him.

As she slipped her flannel dorm shirt over her head, Karen caught a glimpse of herself in the mirror over her dresser. "I look like me again," she whispered, sitting on her bed. The last time she had seen her reflection was in the lounge at work, when she had put on Estelle's extra uniform. No wonder Mr. Chrystal mistook her for her mother — she looked practically twenty in that skirt and blouse.

The artificial Karen was gone, but the old Karen wasn't exactly the same, either. The knowledge of some secret — whatever it was — between her mother and Alexander Chrystal had rudely catapulted Karen to a new level of adulthood she wasn't sure she was ready for.

Horatio bumped his head against her knee, purring loudly, then gave her ankle a little love nip.

"Want some attention, big boy?" She hauled the heavy yellow cat into her lap, where he hung over in every direction, kneading his tiger paws. When he dug too hard into her leg, she yelled, "Ouch!" and unceremoniously shoved him to the floor.

"You go too far," she chided the cat, who stood with his back to her, his striped coat rippling with annoyance.

"Oh, Horatio, why can't things stay the same?" she whispered.

His neck stiff with dignity, Horatio turned to stare at her, green eyes disdainful slits, as if to say, "I know why things change, but I'm not about to tell *you!*"

Suddenly Karen remembered the pin in her jewelry box. Almost from the moment the pin found its way into her hand, her life had been plunged into chaos. She'd discovered it the evening of the disastrous triple date, and she'd later learned her father was out of work. The pin was a bad omen, but where had it come from?

There was her opening. She would ask her mother about the pin and gradually lead into the incident with Chelsea's parents. Perhaps she could solve two mysteries at once. With what little bravery she could summon she left her room, clutching the cougar pin.

The kitchen was a warm and cozy cocoon, wrapped in the dark silence of the rest of the house. Johnny wasn't home yet, though it was nearly midnight, and her father undoubtedly had gone to bed early. He'd been sleeping a lot lately, getting up later and later in the mornings, turning in earlier and earlier, and even taking naps in the afternoons. Sleeping his life away, Karen thought, then immediately chastised herself for judging her father so harshly. It wasn't his fault the Chrystal dynasty decided to lay off workers at the mill. And it certainly wasn't his fault he couldn't get another job in the meantime.

"The cocoa is almost ready. Sit down." Her mother opened a cabinet and took out a bag of marshmallows. "I thought we needed a treat. Life isn't worth living if you can't have marshmallows in your hot chocolate." She smiled warmly.

"Here we are," Gloria said now, setting the steaming mug before Karen. She dropped three marshmallows into Karen's cup with a flourish, then gave her a spoon, remembering Karen liked to dunk her marshmallows until they melted into creamy foam, mingling deliciously with the semi-sweet chocolate drink.

When Gloria set her own cup at her place and sat down, Karen peered over and asked, "Why didn't you put more marshmallows into yours?"

"I only wanted one."

"You gave me three. Why didn't you take three? You know Johnny will just eat them tomorrow before breakfast."

Her mother frowned. "I said I only wanted one. What is *wrong* with you tonight?"

"Nothing," Karen answered lamely. "It's just that I get tired of seeing you do without things . . . even silly things like marshmallows."

"I don't do without, as you say. In case you haven't noticed, I'm not as young as I used to be. Not as thin. I'm at that age where I have to watch my weight and three marshmallows is a luxury my hips can't afford."

Through the fragrant steam of her chocolate, Karen watched her mother pick up her own cup. Gloria Pickett's hands were small, like a child's, yet there was nothing childlike in the way those capable fingers managed a family and a household, even one in trouble. Everyone remarked how Karen resembled her mother — they had the same brown hair and eyes, and though her mother was a little heavier and curvier, they were about the same size. They also had the same ability to face life head on.

Karen pulled the class pin from the pocket of her bathrobe and set it on the table. "I found this in the jewelry box you gave me. Is it yours?"

Gloria's hand trembled slightly as she picked it up. "Yes, it's mine," she admitted cautiously. "I'd nearly forgotten about it."

"Is it a school pin? It's got the Chrystal Falls cougar on it — and the school colors." Karen paused.

"Well . . ." Gloria regarded the pin as though it were the key to a door she'd never been able to open. "Yes, it's a school pin. They only made these a few years, I guess. Varsity pins they were called. Guys wore them on their letter jackets."

"Some guy gave this to you? Was it Dad?" Please let it be Daddy, Karen prayed. But she knew it wasn't.

"Yes, someone gave it to me and no, it wasn't your father."

"Tell me about him." Karen sipped her rapidly-cooling cocoa casually, but her stomach fluttered as she remembered Alexander Chrystal's unsettling gaze.

Gloria folded her hands around her cup and gazed into it, as though conjuring the boy's image in the swirling brown liquid. "He was very handsome and very popular. Star of the football team. Class president. The lead in *Oklahoma!* Every girl in school was crazy about him."

"Including you?"

Her mother's laugh echoed nostalgia. "Including me. I worshipped him from afar, as they say. It was pointless to even be infatuated with this boy. He'd never look twice at me. He was older, and out of my league. But one day, he looked across a crowded room and saw me, just like in the song. And that was the beginning."

"He gave you his pin, so he must have been serious," Karen interrupted.

"Oh, he was. In fact, we were going to be married."

Marriage! "What happened? Why did you break up? Was it Daddy? Did you meet Daddy then and fall in love with him instead?" Karen wanted the answer to be *yes*.

"No, I didn't meet Carl till a few years later. We broke up because — because his family didn't approve of me. I wasn't suitable. Not for their son. You see, he was . . .

important and he needed a wife who was . . . the proper kind of girl."

Karen couldn't stand it another second. Outraged, she blurted, "Chelsea's mother can't hold a candle to you! And Alexander Chrystal wasn't worth it anyway! He's just a snob. The whole family are snobs."

Her mother stared at her. "What are you talking about? Who said anything about Alexander?"

"You didn't have to. *He* gave you this pin, didn't he? He was the handsome, popular boy who threw you over because he thought you weren't good enough."

"Stop, Karen. Back up. How did you know it was Alexander Chrystal? I never mentioned his name."

"He came into the dining room tonight. With his wife. They sat at one of my tables. When he saw me, he said 'Gloria.'" She imitated the tender tone he had used. "Just like that. It was creepy, almost. Then he tried to cover it up by telling me I looked like someone he once knew."

"Oh, no." Her mother covered her mouth. "What did Elizabeth do?"

"Nothing. Like I said, he covered it up very smoothly. Mom, did you really love Chelsea's father? How could you fall in love with somebody like *him*?"

"You have to remember it was all a long time ago," her mother reminded her. "He wasn't Chelsea's father then. And I wasn't your mother. I was seventeen, a year older than you are now. And I believed he was the most wonderful boy in the whole world."

"But you were going to marry him! And he left you!"

"Not exactly. I was hurt, yes. I thought he was the only man I'd ever love, that I'd ever want to marry. But I managed to get over it, Karen. I met your father and fell in love again. Broken hearts *do* mend. I've been happy with your father. We've had some hard times, but we love each other and in the end, that's all that really matters."

The truth was worse than Karen had ever imagined. Had her mother had an affair with Chelsea's father? She didn't want to even think about it. But she asked suddenly, "What would it have been like, do you think, if you had married Mr. Chrystal?"

Her mother chose not to answer that question. "It's after twelve, Karen. Go on to bed."

The front lobby of Chrystal Falls High looked like the entrance of any high school in the country. Built-in glass cases displayed trophies and other awards, announcing the Cougars' latest triumphs. Brass signs directed visitors to the office. There was a drinking fountain, known colloquially as the Freshman Watering Hole, where underclassmen congregated, striving to be noticed by juniors and seniors who barely looked at them.

In the center of the lobby floor was a tile mosaic. It depicted a stalking cougar against a background of burgundy and gold, the school symbol. The mosaic was a gift from the Class of '59, who crafted the picture from bits of broken tiles, working on it one solid year while new flooring was being installed.

From her very first day of high school, Karen regarded the mosaic as something too beautiful to be stepped on, so she made a point to go around the cougar whenever she entered the building. Not stepping on the mosaic became a talisman to her. If she kept her pledge, good things would happen to her. Occasionally, she'd be forced to break her rule — someone would bump into her or the lobby would be so jammed, she'd have no choice but to tramp on the cougar.

This morning, the cougar was a life-sized reminder of the truth she'd learned last night. This cougar looked exactly like the tiny cougar engraved on her mother's class pin. Alexander Chrystal's pin, Karen amended silently.

Karen broke her private vow. She stepped squarely on the cougar's face on her way to her first class.

In gym, she was so off-stride in basketball, the other team crushed hers, a shameful 23-46. The locker room teasing she received was merciless.

"So, the great Karen Pickett actually lost?" a laughing voice came across the locker room. "Quick! Somebody rush this to the *Chrystal Falls Clarion* — 'Star Athlete Dribbles Her Last Ball.'"

Karen was in no mood for joking. "Lay off," she warned the girl.

A silk camisole drifted over Chelsea Chrystal's head for a split second, then her shining cap of hair popped into view. "Now, Karen," she teased. "You should accept defeat like a good sport. Of course, we realize this is a totally new experience."

Chelsea didn't mean to be hurtful any more than the other girls did, but it was all Karen could do to keep from slapping that perfect face. Would she forever be plagued by Chrystals? "Shut up, Chelsea."

Dawn, who had finished dressing, gave Karen one of her come-on-can't-you-guys-be-friends looks. "Karen —"

"It's okay, Dawn," Chelsea said. "Karen's probably tired. The dining room at the club was pretty busy last night." Thanks to you, Karen thought bitterly. "It's hard to be pleasant when you're wiped out."

Karen despised Chelsea defending her. "You want pleasant?" she said to Chelsea, her voice shaking. "I'll give you pleasant. How pleasant was your father when he dumped my mother twenty years ago?"

"What are you talking about? My *father* dumping your *mother*? Did she work at our house or something?"

"No, she wasn't a servant! My mother and your father were in love! They were engaged!"

There was a sudden, total silence in the locker room.

"What did you say?" Chelsea breathed, those marvelous aquamarine eyes registering disbelief.

"I *said* your father was in love with my mother!" Karen enjoyed watching the changing expressions on Chelsea's face. "They probably had an affair!"

"It's a lie!"

"Chelsea . . . Karen . . . please," Dawn said, coming over to stand between them as if she expected them to physically fight any minute.

"It's not a lie, Chelsea Chrystal," Karen said. "You want proof? Ask your father. Why don't you? At dinner tonight ask your father why he left the first girl he ever loved."

Chapter Seven

As she drove home from school, Chelsea's hands numbly gripped the leather racing cover of the steering wheel. She had managed to get through the rest of her classes in typical Chelsea Chrystal style, but it was only an act. She'd been rocked to the core by Karen's accusation, though she wouldn't give Karen or the other girls in the locker room the satisfaction of seeing that.

The show must go on, she resolved. And Chelsea put on a brilliant performance. After Karen dropped her bombshell, Chelsea denied it coolly, finished dressing as though she had all the time in the world, instead of a scant two minutes before the next bell, and then strolled to her French class, head held high, bantering with Ryan and his friends. To all appearances, Chelsea Chrystal was unruffled by the allegation Karen Pickett had made in the locker room. She hoped she had successfully squelched any more vicious gossip right there, before it flashed through school like an out-of-control brush fire.

Yet when the last bell rang and Perky asked Chelsea to join her and Hollis at the country club, Chelsea declined, claiming she had a big test to study for. The truth was she couldn't have carried on the pretense another second.

My father, she thought, turning the car into the driveway, in love with Gloria Pickett! Karen Pickett's mother! A milltown girl! A girl who must have been so different from her father.

As she spun the car into her customary parking space, she noticed the silver Cadillac with the license plate that read "CRSTL-3." So her mother was home.

Chelsea sat in her car a few minutes, bundled against the November chill in her full-length down coat, her hands knotted in her lap. Her tape deck played an old Elton John cassette, but she didn't hear a single note. Unrelated thoughts whirled through her mind . . . Daddy . . . Mother . . . Karen . . . Gloria Pickett. . . .

A blustery wind lashed the towering oaks that flanked the Chrystal mansion. Dead leaves scattered over the lawn, collecting in temporary bunches, and then were blown apart. Shriveled flowers along the driveway, not yet removed by the groundskeeper who tended the lawn and gardens, bowed their heads on withered stems, as if too weary to face the coming winter.

The house on the hill, standing in the failing autumn light, had an air of abandonment.

Chelsea knew that wasn't so. Her mother and grandmother Lillian and Amy were home, along with the household staff. The Judge and her grandmother were getting ready to go to Palm Springs for a few weeks, but they weren't leaving until tomorrow. Then why did she suddenly feel orphaned? A shiver rippled across her shoulder blades, and she burrowed into her coat.

Someone walking across my grave, she thought automatically, then roused herself. This is silly! You are *not* alone — your mother and father love you *and* each other dearly and they always have. Karen Pickett was just being nasty. Or was she? There was only one way to find out. . . .

"Hi, Mom," Chelsea said as cheerfully as she could, finding her mother sitting at the antique desk in the sun room, her checkbook open.

Elizabeth Chrystal offered a smooth, porcelain-pale cheek to her daughter. "Hello, darling. How was school?"

Chelsea's heart gave a suspicious skip. Did her mother know something already? "Why do you ask?"

"Because I always ask," her mother replied. "And usually you give me a better answer than that."

"Sorry. It was fine. Okay." Chelsea tossed her coat over the back of the love seat and scooted the ottoman closer to her mother's desk. "What's new?"

Elizabeth's gold Mark Cross pen checked off a column of figures. "Chelsea, dear, how many times have I told you to hang up your coat, not throw it all over the furniture."

"Marie will hang it up," Chelsea said, referring to the housekeeper.

"Marie has more important duties than picking up after you."

"I'll hang it up in a minute." Chelsea toyed with the zipper on her boot, marshaling her jumbled thoughts into a leading question. "Mom, when you met Dad, was it love at first sight?"

"For him or for me?"

She hadn't thought of it that way. "For both of you."

"Well, I really can't speak for Alex, but I was attracted to your father the first time I met him."

"Yes, but did you love him?"

Now her mother put down her pen. "Actually, no. Love came later, the way it's supposed to. You don't really believe that people can fall in love instantly, do you?" She peered closely at her daughter. "You haven't gone and fallen head over heels for another guitar-playing Lothario like you did last year?"

Chelsea felt a rush of embarrassment. Would her mother ever forget the crush she had had on that local rock musician?

"Heavens, Mother, I was only a child."

"Two years older than Amy is now," her mother pointed out wryly. "And I suppose that at sixteen you are a woman of the world?"

This wasn't going at all the way she planned. "I just want to know about you and Daddy. About your courtship days. Was he the first man you ever loved?"

"Honestly, Chelsea, do we have to go into this right now? I am trying to unsnarl the hospital charity fund account that Dolly Palmer left in an absolute muddle, and you're asking these ridiculous questions!"

"Just answer yes or no, Mom. Please. Was Dad the first man you ever loved?" Chelsea used her most winning voice, the one she relied upon to wheedle a new cashmere sweater from her mother or father.

"I can't see what possible difference it makes to you, but the answer is yes. Alex was my first love."

"Were you *his* first love?" Chelsea persisted.

But her mother had run out of patience. "Chelsea, are you doing a report for school or something? A social studies essay on courtship and marriage? I must finish these books before dinner."

"Please, Mother. Just answer this and I promise I'll go away and leave you alone." She hoped her mother wouldn't hear her heart thudding against her rib cage.

Elizabeth switched on her calculator. The machine hummed faintly but persistently, a subtle reminder that nothing would interrupt the business at hand for very long. She turned away from Chelsea and began clicking the keys with the flat part of her fingers, so as not to chip her perfectly manicured nails.

"Mom? What about Dad? Were you the first girl he ever loved?"

"I think you ought to ask him." Elizabeth's words clipped in time with the striking of the calculator keys.

The audience was over. Chelsea picked up her coat and hung it in the closet, a sick feeling growing in the pit of her stomach, like an inkstain spreading over a white velvet sofa. Suppose what Karen said was true? That her father *did* love Karen's mother once, before he met Elizabeth?

For the first time in her life, Chelsea Chrystal had a wonderful piece of gossip and it wasn't the least bit delicious. Ordinarily, she was excited by other people's secrets, not exactly feeding off them, but relishing gossip with the zest of someone who appreciated the little obstacles life threw in one's path. As long as those things happened to other people.

Now it wasn't thrilling at all.

In her room, Chelsea put on the TV. She needed noise, anything mindless to drive away the thoughts that battered at her like hailstones.

A knock sounded. Amy stuck her head through the door. "Can I come in?"

"I guess so," Chelsea said reluctantly. "What do you want?"

"Nothing. I thought maybe you wanted to

go riding or something." Amy never seemed to care how cold it was outside. She rode her precious Appaloosa in all kinds of weather, at any hour of the day. She would have ridden at midnight, if she thought she could get away with it.

"In case you haven't noticed, Amy, it's freezing outside. No, I don't want to go riding." Listlessly, Chelsea sifted through her video cassette library. Maybe a film would help, a mystery or a sprawling Western. Definitely no love stories.

"Okay. Let's watch a movie then." Amy sat cross-legged on the floor beside Chelsea, eagerly going through the case that held Chelsea's collection of cassettes. *"The Sound of Music!* I love that one. I'll put it in." She leaned over and slid the cassette into the VCR.

Chelsea pushed the eject button angrily, snatching the tape from the machine. "No! I don't want to watch a movie. I've changed my mind." In truth, she adored *The Sound of Music* as much as Amy did, but today she couldn't bear to watch prim Julie Andrews steal Christopher Plummer away from the beautiful Baroness. She always imagined the actress who played the rich Baroness Schraeder looked like her mother — regal, blond, perfect down to the last hair on her head. Gracious even when jilted.

Amy was staring at her with those dark eyes she inherited from grandmother Lillian. "Okay, Chels. We won't watch a movie. Whatever you say." She appeared to put aside her own hurt feelings as she asked, "Is something wrong, Chels? Are you sick?"

"No." But she was. Because just then another dreadful thought occurred to her. Suppose her father and Karen's mother were *still* in love, even though they were married to other people. What if they were having a love affair right this very minute, behind her mother's back?

"Maybe you ought to —" Amy began, but Chelsea leaped up, pulling her sister with her.

"Amy, I really don't want you in my room. Will you get out and leave me alone?" Chelsea had never spoken to Amy this harshly before and the words hurt her throat even as she said them. But she couldn't bear to look at her sister, an innocent thirteen-year-old, who had no idea of how faithless people could be. Amy also adored her father, steadfastly believing he was the most wonderful man in the universe. She couldn't risk Amy finding out. She pretended not to see the hurt in Amy's eyes as she silently left the room.

Chelsea pressed her fists against her temples. I can't stand this! She needed a diversion. The best diversion she could think of was Josh Newhouse, a tantalizing six-footer with wavy dark hair that would make any normal girl forget her troubles. Yes, that's exactly what she needed. Of course, she only knew Josh as Dawn's brother, a friend who often looked at her as though he wanted to get to know her better. Because they were nowhere near the stage where she could snap her fingers and he'd come running, she called Perky and asked her to come over.

"What's up?" Perky said when she arrived. "I thought you had a big test to study for." Her icycle-blue eyes glittered more than usual this evening.

"I do."

The corners of Perky's mouth turned down. "I hope you didn't call me over to help you study. What's the subject?"

"Josh Newhouse."

Perky brightened. "A new battle plan, huh?"

"You guessed it." Chelsea managed a smile. "He interests me . . . a lot."

Perky settled down on the rug, making herself comfortable. "I don't blame you a bit. That Josh is one sexy guy. He sure beats the pants off Ryan in tennis. I wonder what else he's a pro at. Speaking of Josh, have you heard about Dawn?"

Chelsea had a vague memory of Dawn calling to her the other day after the fire drill. "We didn't get a chance to talk in gym today." Other things came up, she thought grimly. "What about Dawn?"

"She's starting up again with Pete Carter! Can you believe it? I saw them talking in the hall today, *tres* intimate! You wait, before the holidays are here, Dawn and Pete will be an item. Poor Ian."

"What do you mean 'poor?' Don't tell me you aren't planning to be there when Ian needs a shoulder to cry on."

"We'll see. But don't you think it's terrible that Dawn Newhouse still is running after a milltowner? What's wrong with that girl anyway? You'd think she'd know better. I guess it's the old forbidden-fruit theory. The grass always looks greener on the wrong side of the tracks." Perky grinned.

With chilling insight, Chelsea knew what was coming next. She'd been friends with Perky Palmer too many years not to know how her mind worked.

Perky leaned against the ottoman, stretching casually. "By the way, Chels. I heard an interesting tidbit. It seems I missed all the fireworks in gym today. How come you didn't tell me what happened?"

"What's there to tell?" Chelsea asked, dreading Perky's answer.

"I heard Karen zapped you with the most incredible statement. Something about your father and her mother being old lovers?"

"Who told you that?" Chelsea whispered.

Perky smiled cruelly. She loved being in what she considered a position of power. "Why, Chels, it's all over school. Your father and Gloria Pick —"

Like a rubber band wound too tightly, Chelsea snapped. She heaved a pillow at Perky. "I don't need to hear this from you, Palmer! I thought you were my friend. Get out of here before I say what I really think of you!"

"Don't yell at me, Chelsea. I only told you what I heard."

"And probably spread all over town. Get out!" Chelsea shouted.

Perky left quickly. Chelsea shut the door behind her, then sagged against it, exhausted. Her worst fears were confirmed — before the night was over, everyone in Chrystal Falls would know about her father and Gloria Pickett. Damn that Karen!

When the phone rang, Chelsea jumped. She picked up the receiver. "Hello?" she said warily.

There was a staticky pause. Then, "Hello, Chelsea." A strange voice, somewhat hushed but throbbing with thinly-veiled excitement. The same man who had called the other night.

"Who are you?" she demanded.

He ignored this. "What are you doing tonight, Chelsea? I bet you're going to a fancy party, aren't you? What are you going to wear?"

Chelsea felt her apprehension thaw into fascination. His voice sounded oddly familiar, like a personality on television. Or a boy from school. Intrigued, she asked, "Why do you care what I'm doing tonight?"

"I'm interested in everything you do," the caller replied. "Tell me where you're going. Are you going to wear that pretty blue dress?"

"Which blue dress? I've got dozens," she answered flippantly, falling under the spell of his husky voice. It's probably some boy from school, she decided. That's it. Some cute shy boy with a huge crush on me, playing this silly game. Okay. She'd play along. "You mean that blue dress with the thin straps?"

"That's the one," the caller agreed. "The short one. Shows off your pretty shoulders."

"Thank you." Chelsea made her voice reflect the dimpled smile her secret admirer couldn't see. "Why won't you tell me who you are? Just give me a hint."

"You'll see me soon enough."

"Really? In school?" She was practically dying of curiosity. "Or at the country club? I go there almost every —"

"Good-bye, Chelsea. See you around."

He hung up on that note, his last words echoing in her ear. Was it her imagination or did he sound just a shade sinister? No. She was simply upset over all that business about her father and Karen's mother.

Whoever this man was, he was obviously head-over-heels crazy about her. Nothing wrong with that. A girl could never have too many admirers. He was a distraction, something that kept her from concentrating on her father. Chelsea had seen Gloria Pickett around town many times. She was pretty in a tired kind of way. But her mother was beautiful. Her mother was what Chelsea wished *she* was like . . . always polite, always contained. Her mother would never have flirted with a strange man over the telephone.

Chapter Eight

Dawn paced between the hexagonal mirror hanging in the foyer and the picture window in the living room, checking her appearance one minute, the parking lot the next.

"You look fine," she reassured the image in the mirror, yet a wrinkle of doubt creased her reflection's forehead. She *did* look terrific. Her royal blue quilted jacket brightened her eyes and contrasted sharply with her glossy midnight hair, bringing out blue-black highlights.

Then why the frown?

It was Friday evening and, except for Abner snoring and twitching on the sofa, the apartment was empty. Her mother and Josh were having dinner at Uncle Walt's. Dawn had begged off, pleading an English paper due Monday. Actually, her paper on Thoreau wasn't due for another two weeks, but she needed an excuse.

Tonight she was meeting Pete Carter . . . secretly.

She'd given up a family gathering and a movie afterward with Ian to keep this night free. Dawn didn't mind missing Aunt Vicki's dinner but she felt guilty turning Ian down. She knew she'd hurt his feelings when she told him she already had a date and doubted he would ever try to make another one. Not that she could blame him.

That was what Pete Carter did to her. He made her lie to her mother and act nasty to perfectly nice boys. The anxiety of seeing Pete again kept her shackled to the living room window, broken only by nervous forays into the hall to see that her hair was still smooth and her lipgloss unsmeared.

It was five till eight. Pete said he'd pick her up at seven-thirty. He was late. Or had he changed his mind altogether? With Pete, she could never tell.

The weeks following the hit-and-run accident, when Pete abruptly declared it was over between them, were spent warily avoiding each other in school. Pete shared two classes with her, so not seeing him at all was impossible. Sometimes, in either English or history, she felt his dark eyes on her, burning into her very soul, dragging her eyes up from her textbook to look in his direction. But whenever she glanced over at him, he was always staring out the window or down at his desk.

And then came the fire drill. Out in the

freezing parking lot, Pete's iron-bound reserve loosened — he was definitely still interested in her. That evening, Dawn couldn't wait for supper to end so she could volunteer to walk Abner. She practically raced the dog down to the river, hoping Pete would be there, leaning against the lamppost like the old days, holding out a hand for the jacket he'd loaned her in the school parking lot.

But he wasn't. And she didn't see him the next night, or the next. Dawn was not the type to lose faith. She timed her nightly strolls down to the river with such regularity that Abner was almost getting bored with the routine, but Dawn couldn't risk missing Pete.

On the fourth night, a damp, bone-chilling evening that only November can produce, he was there. As she approached the river, Abner tugged at the leash, straining to hurry his mistress along. When his tail feathered the air and he whimpered, greeting an old friend, Dawn's heart kicked like a trapped rabbit.

Take it easy, she cautioned herself. Go slow. He's as skittish as you are and you don't want to scare him off.

"Hello, Pete."

"Hello yourself, Newhouse." He bent down to scratch Abner behind his thick ruff.

Frantically searching her brain for the safest, most innocent opener she could think of, Dawn finally came up with, "Nice night."

"Yeah, it is. If you like raw, freezing weather."

Now that was a real lead balloon, she moaned inwardly.

He looked so handsome, backdropped by the fog-shrouded river. The soft sodium streetlight illuminated his face into a study of planes and shadows. Dawn would have been content to stare at Pete all night, but Abner chose that moment to wind around their legs, entangling himself and them in his leash.

Suddenly Pete was so close she could feel his breath on her cheek, a sweet, elusive smell like fresh hay in the loft of a barn. She backed up a half a step, nearly tripping over the dog.

"Abner, stop it!" Dawn pulled the leash through their legs so they could move apart.

"He's just glad to be out of that apartment, aren't you? He hates being cooped up. Big dogs like him are meant to run free, out in the country."

"Abner agrees with you and so do I," Dawn said, grateful that the dog gave them something to talk about. "Unfortunately, we can't afford a house here yet. Not on Mom's salary and with two college educations looming in the future."

"College, huh? Where you planning to go?"

Dawn shrugged. "Right here, I guess. At least for two years, then I'll probably go on to State. My mother is a great believer in local colleges and universities." She wanted to get off this subject. Pete was overly sensitive about the fact that her mother was a doctor and that college for Dawn and Josh, while still a tight squeeze, was a definite in their futures. Pete's own future, she suspected, was as undecided and vaporous as the white smoke that hung over the mill.

Though their conversation progressed in fits and starts at first, they did talk for more than a half an hour, until Dawn reluctantly said Josh would be worried if she stayed out any longer.

"I don't blame him," Pete said. "He has a very special sister. Newhouse, I know it's been sort of rough lately —" He stopped, then tentatively took her hand in his, holding it tight, as though she might snatch it back. "I hate to think about the last time we were here ... what I'm trying to say is, would you — do you think we could — ?"

Much as she wanted to just tell him she loved him, she said lightly, "Why don't you ask me out? Let's start from there. Let's start from scratch, as if we were going on a first date. As if nothing ugly or sad had ever happened between us."

Pete pulled her to him and held her against him. "I can't resist you, Newhouse. Just one thing. . . ."

"What?" Dawn murmured against his shoulder.

"I don't want people to know we're seeing each other. I don't want this town part of us. It will just mean more trouble. Will you do that, Newhouse?"

Dawn moved back from him. "How can I lie about where I am when I'm with you?

I've never done anything like that before."

Pete's hands were hard on her shoulders. "Just for a little while. Just until I feel people aren't wondering why a girl like you is with a guy like me."

It wouldn't be easy. Aside from manipulating people and schedules to meet without anyone knowing, they had all the bad times behind them that weren't easily forgotten. But they had decided to try again. Pete's goodnight kiss, warm and tender, had made Dawn know that lying to be with Pete would be worth it.

And now Pete was late. Was he having second thoughts?

Headlights flared, then narrowed to pencil beams outside the window. Her heart leaped with joy, as she recognized Pete's car.

She ran out to meet him. "I wouldn't have been late tonight for a million dollars," he said right away. "But my father was late coming home — and I had to wait for the car."

"That's okay. I understand."

"You do, don't you? I knew you would. You always are loyal, faithful —" He broke off, remembering that *he* had severed their relationship a month ago.

She laughed to break the tension. "You make me sound like a St. Bernard."

He backed the car out of the parking lot, grinning cheerfully. "My best friends happen to be four-footed."

"Where are we going? Someplace to eat, I hope. I'm starved."

"Where would you like to go?"

She tried to keep a wistful note from her voice, but not very successfully. "How about Mom and Pop's?" Before the words left her mouth, she realized she had made a mistake. They were going to start over, from scratch, and here she had suggested going back to their old place.

"I don't think that's such a good idea."

"You're right," Dawn said quickly. "I haven't seen half of this town yet. Surprise me."

"Believe me, if I showed you the other half of town, you'd be surprised," he said dryly.

The last thing Dawn wanted was to start an argument about milltown. "Pizza." She clung to the word as if it were a safety net. "I'm starved for pizza. Know a good place?"

He did. When they were seated in the booth, a red-checked, cloth-covered table between them, Pete ordered a pizza that sounded as authentic as a trip to Rome.

"That was *pizza* you ordered?" Dawn asked.

"The best." He kissed his fingertips in a gesture of heavenly anticipation. "You'll be able to speak fluent Italian when you walk out of here!" Then he sobered. "What's Mac-Farland going to say if he finds out you went out with me tonight?"

"Ian and I are good friends, I told you. That's all. He won't say anything."

"Come on, Newhouse. I've seen the way he looks at you. The man is crazy about you. So are half the guys in school."

"How you do run on, Mr. Carter! Fiddle-dee-dee!" Dawn mimicked Scarlett O'Hara perfectly. "Half the boys crazy about me! Honestly, Pete!"

"Well. . . ." He grinned wickedly. "At least two guys. Out of nine hundred or so boys, that's not such a bad average."

She threw her napkin at him. That was a mistake. She needed that napkin and a dozen more for the gooey, cheesy concoction that came to the table. To Dawn, struggling not to appear as though she'd learned her table manners in Tibet, the iron skillet seemed to hold all the food in the entire Italian restaurant, not one mere pizza.

"You have tomato sauce on your chin," Pete observed.

"I'm amazed it's not on the ceiling." She wiped her face for the forty-third time and mentally made a note never again to eat pizza or spaghetti in front of anyone she wanted to impress.

When the pie was demolished, spaces between their conversation became more pronounced.

"Something is bothering you," Pete observed. "What is it?"

Dawn carefully picked an anchovy off her last bite of pizza. She'd already eaten more anchovies tonight than she'd planned to eat in her entire lifetime. The sacrifices she made for Pete! "It's — it's nothing, really. Forget it."

He reached for her hand. "Don't give me

that. I know what's bugging you — sneaking out with me tonight. Isn't that it?"

She nodded, unable to lie to him. "I felt funny telling Mom and Josh I was going to study this evening."

"It's better this way. At least for now. You're still new here. I don't want people to get the wrong idea about you. If they see you with me. . . ."

They were doing it again. Talking about the early days they had vowed to put aside.

"Stop right there," Dawn said. "What happened to our clean slate? We're supposed to behave like it's our first date, remember?"

"Right. I should be trying to impress you. What's a good way for a guy to get to know a girl?"

Dawn thought of a dozen exciting methods, but she didn't mention them. As much as she wanted to move ahead to the next stage in their relationship, she said primly, "Well, we could tell each other something . . . special . . . about ourselves. How about our most embarrassing moments? You go first."

Pete covered his eyes in mock agony. "Do I have to?"

"Come on. Don't be a spoilsport." Dawn settled back in her chair. She was enjoying this. "I'm waiting."

"I've had a lot of embarrassing moments," Pete stalled.

"Pick one."

He gave in with a sigh. "You asked for it. One time I applied for a junior counselor job at this day camp north of town. I told the guy who ran the camp I had my life-saving badge. I guess he could see right through me because he wanted me to go a few laps around the pool." He paused for effect.

"You didn't have a life-saving badge," Dawn guessed.

"Worse. I couldn't even swim! There were a bunch of guys around the pool egging me on. I couldn't back down. So I stood on the edge, jumped as far across as I could, and then I flailed to the other end. I think I might have walked *over* the water that day, I was so scared!"

Dawn laughed. "How old were you?"

"Fifteen." He grinned to show he was pulling her leg. "No, I was ten or eleven. There was no way that counselor would have hired me. He was just calling my bluff, making me swim."

The picture of a young Pete Carter thrashing across the pool was too wonderful to let go, but Pete said, "Okay, I bared my soul. Now it's your turn."

"I couldn't top that if I tried. Here goes. When Josh was in first grade, Mom and I went to see him in a school program. The first graders were on last and when it was over, Josh announced that his little sister wanted to sing! Well, nobody had left the auditorium yet, so Josh's teacher asked if this great, undiscovered talent would come forward."

"Don't tell me," Pete interrupted. "You were the next Shirley Temple."

"Wrong. I was horribly shy and what's more, I didn't have any front teeth! The only song I knew was 'Little Tommy Tinker.' Josh taught it to me."

"Did you do it?"

She nodded. "Somehow I managed to climb up on that stage and lisp 'Little Tommy Tinker.' Everybody cracked up and I wanted to kill Josh."

Pete laughed appreciatively. "You mean, a big Broadway talent scout didn't rush up to sign you to his next show?"

"If one was in the audience, he ran out the back door."

Swapping childhood reminiscences accomplished more than breaking the ice, Dawn decided. They had shared small pieces of their past with one another, silly things, intimate things, which drew them closer together.

In the parking lot back at her apartment, Pete pulled her into the warm circle of his arms.

"Am I going to see you again?" Dawn asked, suddenly afraid he would dissolve into the night. Did this evening really happen?

Pete's lips on hers, firm but loving, answered her question. "We probably shouldn't, but what the hell. How about tomorrow? Can you get out tomorrow afternoon?"

It wasn't easy but Dawn slipped out after lunch. She met Pete at the river as agreed. He had been waiting for her in the cold for more than an hour.

"I thought you'd never get here," he said, kissing her.

"Me, too." Already Dawn felt the seconds dribbling away, dreading the approach of four o'clock, when she'd have to leave him and go home. Her day hadn't even begun until she was with Pete again and it would be over all too quickly. "I'm here now. What'll we do?"

"Fly a kite."

"You're kidding."

He wasn't. He had bought one of those plastic preassembled kites in the shape of a dragon. They hiked to a high point overlooking the river. Though the November wind was fickle, Pete launched the kite to Dawn's cheers and soon the dragon soared over Rapid River. Once the kite was aloft, he turned his attention to Dawn. They kissed, while the kite bobbed in the breeze. Each kiss was more intense than the one before.

"I wish it could be like this always," Dawn said after a while.

Pete didn't speak. Dawn knew he was thinking of the differences that separated them. Chrystal Falls. Long before she moved here, the town divided, casting its inhabitants into irreversible molds. She wondered how two people could be so very right for each other . . . and yet so wrong.

Overhead, the dragon kite yanked at its string, as if it yearned to break away from earthly bonds.

Chapter Nine

The calls came every night.

Monday:

"Hello, Chelsea." The breathless voice greeted her with easy familiarity. "Going out again tonight?"

"Who is this? Why do you care if I'm going out?" Chelsea kept her tone light and seductive, but she couldn't get the caller to reveal his identity.

"Just curious. Which car are you taking, the snazzy red Porsche or your convertible?"

"How did you know my father let me take the Porsche this weekend? It was the first time —"

"I know a lot about you, Chelsea. And I want to know more."

"Why don't you tell me who —"

"So long, Chels. See you around."

Tuesday:

"Hello, Chelsea. What are you doing?"

"You mean you don't know?"

A mirthless laugh. "I thought I'd let you tell me for a change. Big date tonight?"

"As a matter of fact, no. I don't go out every single night of the week."

"I find that hard to believe. A beautiful girl like you. The guys must be standing in line, aren't they?"

Chelsea could never resist a compliment. "All but one. When are you going to take off your mask? Tell me who you are! Is this Doug Gregoire? Because if it is —"

"Nice try, but it won't work, Chels. When the time is right, you'll know. In the meantime . . . maybe I'll see you around."

Wednesday:

"Hi, there, Chels. What's doing?"

"Don't ask, whoever you are, because I'm tired of playing your stupid little game. If you were a *real* man, you'd —"

The bantering tone was dropped. His voice was tight with anger. "What makes you think I'm not a real man?"

At last, Chelsea thought, I got a rise out of the Lone Ranger. "If you *were* a real man, you wouldn't hide behind the telephone. You'd meet me in person."

"I told you last time we'll meet soon enough. When the time is right."

"And when will that be?"

"When you least expect it. Remember,

Chels, we're playing by my rules."

"What if I don't want to play?"

"Oh, you'll play, all right, little rich girl. You'll play, Chelsea. See you around."

By Thursday, it was no longer a game to Chelsea. The stranger had called eight times in the past two weeks, and every night since Saturday. On Monday, Chelsea decided to write down as much of their conversation as she could remember. Maybe if she had the words down on paper, she could figure out who it was. But mostly, she needed tangible proof she was being harassed. In addition to their dialogue, she also noted the time he called and approximately how long he kept her on the line.

The notebook revealed an appalling pattern.

The man phoned at about the same time every evening, between eleven and eleven-thirty. Chelsea was usually in her room then on school nights. Conversations were less than five minutes, although one lasted about ten minutes, and the stranger always terminated the exchange, even if he had to cut Chelsea off.

And he always ended with the same remark. "See you around."

Taken singly or all together, these peculiarities weren't that sinister. But what had Chelsea terrified on this frigid November morning were the conversations themselves.

Before Monday of this week, Chelsea hadn't

recorded the earlier calls, but she remembered the gist of the exchanges pretty much. The calls she'd received over the weekend seemed harmless and Chelsea had flirted with him outrageously. But something he'd said Sunday night prompted her to put a spiral notebook and a pen by her telephone, anticipating his call Monday night.

"How's your little sister?" he'd asked. "The cute one who rides the spotted horse?" Up until that point, his tone had been soft, if a little husky, but still pleasant. There was a sharp edge now that Chelsea didn't like.

"Why do you want to know about my sister?" she'd countered, but the man only laughed. The laugh bothered Chelsea. After he told her he'd "see her around," she thought about going to her father. Yet she was put off by an unexplained feeling toward the father she'd always loved. Even if the thing with Karen's mother was in the past, long dead and buried, she suddenly didn't trust him . . . didn't feel she could talk to him.

Besides, she rationalized, who'd believe her? She had a private line. No one could pick up one of the half a dozen extensions throughout the house and listen in. She considered taping her caller's conversations — by far the best proof she could offer. But he might know about electronics and have a detection device on his own phone.

That left writing down conversations in a notebook — not as accurate as a tape recording, but better than nothing.

The transcripts of the last three phone calls provided Chelsea with unshakable evidence and confirmed a suspicion that had disturbed her sleep for the past week: she was in trouble.

The caller wasn't anyone from school, she was certain. Nor was it anyone from the country club or Rapid River College. If he was a stranger, he knew her routine, and even what car she drove on a given day, yet he remained furtively in the background, like a shadow one glimpses disappearing around the corner. There, but never seen.

What she dreaded most was the day she *would* see him. His teasing closing remark, which once filled Chelsea with the promise of an exciting, new adventure, now froze her blood.

See you around.

She prayed she wouldn't.

All that day in school, Chelsea was jumpy as a cat. Even Perky, who was almost completely insensitive, noticed how nervous she was.

"You ought to go to the nurse's office and lie down a while," Perky suggested. "You look awful, Chelsea. Like you've seen a ghost."

Maybe I have, Chelsea thought. Mine.

She tried to concentrate on her classes, but the caller's breathy, low-pitched voice kept getting in her way.

You'll play, little rich girl.

When someone grabbed the back of her neck while she was loading books into her locker, she screamed. An ear-splitting cry that caused the other kids to stare at her.

"It's only me, Chelsea." Ryan Simpson spun her around so she could see his face. "What on earth is wrong with you?"

"For God's sake, Ryan. You scared me, that's what's wrong! Don't ever do that again!" She clutched her chest, certain her heart had stopped.

He raised his hands in a gesture of submission. "Okay, okay. Sorry. For a minute there, I thought I'd lost my magic touch."

"What about me? I think I've lost about ten years. Is my hair white?" She angled her head forward.

Ryan ran strong fingers through her shining hair, which she wore in curls today. "Snow-white, I'm afraid. You'd better hit the Peroxide Palace after school for a quick fix."

She giggled, thankful for his normal, joking self. "Peroxide bleaches hair, dumb boy."

He gave her a foolish grin. "Whatever. Don't worry, darling, I'll always love you, white hair, wrinkles, the whole bit."

"Listen, I'll still be gorgeous when I'm pushing you around in a wheelchair." Good old Ryan-to-the-rescue. He revived her flagging self-confidence. Just what she needed.

"Is that so? All right, Grandma. How about you and me going to the Club tonight to gum a hamburger? I'll supply the wheels and denture cream." He took her hand and began to draw slow, lazy circles on her palm, oblivious to the kids streaming past them in the hall.

"How about it, Chels? Want to go out tonight? I haven't seen you in ages."

"Not since Saturday. But I can see your problem. Five whole days without me. Poor baby, what a terrible sacrifice."

Ryan pretended to swoon against the lockers. One thing about Ryan Simpson, she could count on him in a pinch. They'd been friends since their sandbox days. Maybe she *should* go out with him tonight. If she stayed out later than usual, late enough to miss her caller, that would throw him off. Let him know she wasn't sitting around, biting her nails, waiting for his call. Maybe discourage him from calling again.

"Liven up, you lucky boy," she said, punching Ryan's shoulder. "I'll do you a favor and let you take me out, but only on one condition."

"You want me to bring a heating pad for two?"

"Pick me up later than usual. Come by, say, at ten. Or even after."

His forehead crinkled with feigned astonishment. "Ten o'clock for a hamburger? Isn't that kind of late for a school night? What are we going to do — elope?"

She patted his cheek. "You wish."

Ryan was in a jaunty mood when he picked Chelsea up that night. "Ten-fifteen," he said, tapping his imported sports watch. "Late enough for you?"

"Perfect."

They went to the country club. As they

entered the Grill Room, Chelsea's gaze swept the room.

"Looking for somebody?" Ryan teased.

"You know Karen Pickett works here," she said, as they sat down at a booth. "It's hard enough seeing her at school."

Ryan skimmed the menu. "I wish they'd add something new here once in a while. Just to break the monotony. Well, you're in luck, Chels. I don't see Karen. Maybe it's her night off. Or maybe she had to cover for her mother while she slipped out on a date."

Chelsea slapped the menu from his hands, her eyes blazing. "That's enough, Ryan Simpson. I don't want to hear you mention Karen's mother or my father in the same breath ever again. You got me?"

He gave a nonchalant shrug. "Who said anything about your father? I merely stated —"

"I know exactly what you were leading up to. I'm sick to death of gossip! That's all I hear at school."

Ryan hooted. "Quite a switch. You, sick of gossip! Funny how you suddenly turn self-righteous when the dirt concerns your family."

"Ryan, you say one more word and I'll dump this water on your head."

Like Perky, Ryan knew how far to push Chelsea. The look she gave him bordered on murder. "All right. I promise I won't mess with you anymore. Let's order. I'm about to faint from hunger and it's all your fault, making me wait so late to eat."

"Why didn't you eat something earlier,

dummy?" She glanced at the clock over the arcade nook. Twenty of eleven. They would stay here another hour. By the time she got home it would be after midnight. By then her caller would have unsuccessfully tried to reach her. If her mother or Amy happened to hear the phone ringing, they would answer it, maybe frighten off the caller.

"Why the deep study?" Ryan said. "You seem more than a little distracted, Chels. In fact, you've looked like a space cadet for days. Is it this Karen business?"

"No. I thought you weren't going to bring that up again."

He winced. "Sorry. But I am concerned about you. Won't you tell Uncle Ryan what's troubling you, little girl?"

She considered. It would be such a relief to unburden herself to someone. Maybe he could give her some advice. Taking a deep breath, she plunged ahead. "There's this guy calling me. Every night."

"What's so unusual about that? Guys have been calling you since they were old enough to dial a telephone."

"This is different. This guy says weird things."

"Obscene?"

"No. Nothing like that. He asks what am I doing that night. What I'm wearing. What car I'm driving. That sort of thing."

Ryan frowned. "I still don't see the problem. Guys are always calling to ask what you're doing that night." He sighed dramatically.

"It's the heavy price you beautiful females have to pay."

"You don't understand. It's not *what* he says — it's *how* he says it. He gives me the creeps, Ryan. And he won't tell me who he *is*."

Their hamburgers came. Ryan slathered mustard over his, saying, "I bet it's John Archer. That guy's been a jerk since the day he was born. What do you expect from a guy who wears white socks? He's just rattling your chain, Chels. I wouldn't worry about it."

"It's not John Archer! It's not anybody I know. That's the whole point!"

"You're making a mountain out of a molehill, Chelsea. It's some guy from school playing games. They do it all the time. Don't you think if there was something to worry about, I'd worry, too?" He reached over and patted her hand. "Come on, Chels, lighten up."

Chelsea knew Ryan would be no help. But then who was?

By the time Chelsea got home, she was ready to weep from frustration. Ryan hadn't believed her, even when she told him about her notebook. If he wouldn't believe her — a boy she'd known forever — how would her parents react? Was there anyone she could turn to? She felt more alone than she ever had in her life.

Maybe she didn't have a problem anymore, she suddenly thought. Maybe the caller had gotten bored, found someone else to torment.

The phone jangled. Chelsea glanced at the clock on her nightstand. Twelve-fifteen. The latest he'd ever called. She knew it was him.

She had to answer it. Listening to the endless ringing was worse than knowing who was on the other end.

"Hello?" she said, wearily.

"It won't work, Chelsea. You can stay out as late as you want with your rich boyfriends, but I can always get to you. Just remember that."

"Stop calling me! Please. Please, stop. I'm going to get my number changed so you won't be able to call me ever again!"

His laugh was mocking. "Like I said, pretty one, I can *always* get to you. Have you ever broken a leg? An accident on the tennis court or the ski slope? No? You've been real lucky then. I'm afraid your luck's run out, though. Well, it's beddy-bye time. See you around, Chels."

She let the receiver dangle from her lifeless fingers, her heart pounding against her chest. The dial tone purred ominously.

There was no doubt in her mind. He was beyond pestering her over the phone.

Now he wanted to hurt her.

She sank down on the floor, rested her head against the side of her bed, and wept softly.

Chelsea jerked awake at dawn that morning, struggling to free herself from the clutches of a nightmare. Even though her bedside clock read four-thirty, it was graveyard-dark and very still, the stark digital numbers standing out in eerie relief against the ink-blackness of her room. That was all she could see, the blue-outlined four, three, and the zero which flipped to one while she stared. Four-thirty-one.

Quickly Chelsea reached over and switched on her lamp. A triangle of light fell on the familiar objects of her night table. The book she was reading for English, her clock, a tumbler of water, now stale with bubbles. And her telephone.

It sat there, looking innocent enough, neatly contained within its ivory plastic case, the touch-tone buttons in precise rows like tiny tombstones.

Stop, Chelsea ordered herself. It's just a telephone. Nothing more.

But in her dream, the phone had become a monstrous enemy, floating through the air, the receiver reaching out to wrap its coiling cord around and around her neck, tighter and tighter, until she couldn't choke out a single gasp. And on the other end of the twisting snakelike cord, a horrible bloated face loomed before her. . . .

She'd jumped up then, brushing her bangs off her forehead, breathing hard and fast. Her first impulse was to run to her mother, crawl in bed with her. But her mother wasn't there — she had gone to Philadelphia for a few days.

As she sat there, knees drawn up to her chin, Chelsea pondered the meaning of the nightmare. It wasn't merely a nocturnal reflection of her anxieties, she knew, dredging up the feeble scraps of psychology she'd learned in school. No. This dream was a warning, a premonition. Something terrible was going to happen to her.

He had called again last night. Panic-stricken, Chelsea fumbled with her pen and notebook, scribbling down what he said.

"How you doing, Chels? Staying home tonight, I see."

"I'm not going to listen to you anymore. I'm hanging up."

"You do and I'll call right back. I'll ring and ring and ring until you're half-crazy, so you might as well listen, baby. How does it feel to have your perfect life messed up a little?"

"*Why me?*" Chelsea cried out. "Why are you doing this to *me?* What have I ever done to you? I don't even know you. Leave me alone!"

"What have you done to me? Plenty. You'll find out soon enough. See you around, baby. See you someday *real* soon."

Now, as her digital clock ticked off the minutes, Chelsea pushed away the last terrifying remnants of her nightmare and weighed her options. The phone calls were driving her mad. She tried leaving the phone off the hook, but after ten minutes of dial tone, the phone company turned on a shrill beep-beep-beep recording that was intolerable. She didn't have a plug-in jack like many of the extension phones downstairs — her phone was wired firmly into a wall plate. She considered having her number changed, a process that might take a few days and would require some explanation to her father. But even if she threw her phone out the window — a thought that had crossed her mind more than once — what good would it do? He was *out there*, watching her. How else could he monitor her comings and goings? He knew exactly where to find her. And when she was all alone.

She sat up with the light on until it was her normal rising time. As she dressed, she wished desperately she had someone to confide in. If only her grandparents weren't off on that golf trip. If only her mother hadn't gone to Philadelphia. . . . If only she felt she could trust her father again. If only, if only. She could smother in "if onlys."

When Amy came in, kicking the pleats of her new plaid skirt, Chelsea almost broke down and told her. But one look at her sister's freshly scrubbed face, eager to start the day, and Chelsea changed her mind. Amy was too young to share this load — there was nothing she could do to help. And Chelsea didn't want to frighten her.

I'm scared enough as it is, she thought, steering her car out of the driveway. Beside her on the leather seat was the notebook in which she'd transcribed the phone calls, a grim reminder that it was only a scant fifteen hours or so until he called again.

During the assembly that took the place of Chelsea's math class, she sat sandwiched between Perky and Hollis, who poked her and made comments about the principal's speech.

Chelsea paid no attention to them. Nor did she hear the principal. Instead, she was acutely aware of the hundreds of students packed into the auditorium, surrounding her on all sides, closing her in. Could one of them be watching her right now? Noting what she was wearing, who she was sitting with, so he could parrot this information back to her later tonight in his husky, terrorizing voice?

"I'm going to the ladies' room," Chelsea whispered to Perky. "See you in gym in a little while."

As Chelsea hurried up one aisle, she glimpsed a small, dark-haired figure rushing up the other aisle, several yards ahead of her. Karen Pickett, Chelsea observed dully, then dismissed the other girl from her troubled thoughts.

The girls' room was empty. Chelsea pulled a comb through her short hair, astounded by her pallid, pinched image in the mirror. She touched the blue-veined skin under one eye wonderingly. When she had hastily put on her makeup this morning, she hadn't noticed how bad she looked.

This is what he is doing to me.

Suddenly the empty bathroom became a menacing place. Chelsea felt unreasonably frightened alone in the tiled room, just as she'd been claustrophobic in the crowded auditorium. Weak November sunlight filtered uncertainly through the pebbled-glass windows high along one wall. She imagined a face peering down at her, his features distorted by the uneven glass, wicked, leering, barely human. . . .

Scraping her brush and lipsticks into her purse, Chelsea fled the ladies' room, just as the auditorium doors opened wide. The assembly was over. Kids flowed into the hall. A group of freshman boys plowed into Chelsea, knocking her books from her arms. Chelsea flinched as if someone had fired a gun.

"I'll pick them up," she told one of the boys, who was scrambling after her books and papers before they were trampled to pieces. "Just go on."

Unwilling to chance another incident like that, Chelsea huddled in a niche between the corridor and a bank of lockers, waiting until she could walk to the gym without being jostled or touched by anyone else.

Chapter
Ten

Alone in the gym, Karen bounced a basketball against the backboard, not caring if the ball went through the hoop or not. Her P.E. class didn't start for another fifteen minutes. Karen had cut an assembly to come here early, unable to sit in the auditorium while the principal droned on about the overcrowded parking lot. She was certain every eye in the auditorium was on her. As she half-ran up the aisle, she imagined whispers trailing after her.

Her life had become unbearable, and it was partly her own fault. In the car this morning, Johnny tried to shake her from her depression.

"Stop beating your head against a brick wall," he said. "What happened, happened. You can't take it back or make it go away. You have to face it, Karen."

"If only I hadn't blurted it out like that in front of everyone," Karen said dismally.

"Even if I *was* mad at Chelsea, I shouldn't have told her about Mom and Mr. Chrystal. Now the whole town knows. Poor Mom. I've ruined her life. And Dad's."

"You haven't ruined anyone's life. Mom's handling it pretty well, considering," Johnny allowed. "She's a strong lady, she doesn't buckle under easily. And as for Dad, he already knew about Mom and — Monty's father. Mom's not the type to hide things from Dad. *You're* the one who's falling apart."

"I can't help it, I feel so *awful.*"

"Well, quit laying your guilt on other people. Our house is like World War Three these days, what with Dad picking at every little thing I do and you crying in your pillow all the time."

"I do not cry in my pillow," Karen said angrily. "And how would you know if I did — you're never around."

Johnny was really right, Karen decided now, letting the ball roll down the court and going to sit on the bleachers. The Pickett house was like an army barracks in a strange country, where people ate and slept in shifts, yet no one spoke the same language. Johnny stayed out all day and well into the night, working part-time and hanging around with his disreputable friends the rest of the time. Their mother seldom went out, except to the grocery store or to run errands. Although Mrs. Pickett never complained, Karen suspected her mother met with comments and stares wherever she went. Her father had sunk into

119

television oblivion. The TV was his escape from the bills piling up.

Karen contributed almost every penny of her salary to the family, and so did Johnny, but it wasn't enough, even with her father's unemployment insurance. She had seen the unopened notices from the bank that held the mortgage to their house. For the first time, Karen was truly afraid they would lose the house. If that happened, it would surely kill her father, who had worked so hard over the years to buy the little house. Most mill workers were content to rent company housing, but not Carl Pickett. "They don't call it the American dream for nothing," he used to say during the years he worked overtime to save for the house. "There's nothing like owning your own home." And now his greatest source of pride, outside of his family, might be snatched away.

As bad as things were, she had gone and made them worse by lashing out at Chelsea, telling her — and every girl in the locker room — about Chelsea's father's old love affair. From that moment on, her life at school had become hell. Kids whispered about her in the halls and in the cafeteria. The one place no one bothered her was the gymnasium. This was Karen's turf — anyone who crossed her on the volleyball court or the hockey field would have to suffer the consequences.

But lately, the power that surged through her arms and legs, the high she experienced whenever she played any sport, seemed to be leaking away. She felt empty, out of it, as if she were viewing the world through the wrong end of a telescope.

Publicly exposing the truth about her mother and Chelsea's father was like dropping a stone down a bottomless well. Until the stone hit bottom, the repercussions would never end.

"Karen, hi." Dawn swept into the gym. "I see you left the assembly early, too. Wasn't it a crashing bore? Sometimes I think they make us sit through those things as part of an endurance test."

Karen stood in the middle of the scuffed wooden floor. She couldn't even rally enough energy to answer Dawn.

Dawn paused in the doorway of the locker room. "What's wrong, Karen? You look terrible. Come in here with me while I get dressed. I think you need to talk."

Karen sat on the long bench beneath the lockers for lack of anything better to do. Dawn sat down beside her. "We have a few minutes before the mob pours in. Tell me what's bothering you. Is it your father?"

"It's my father. My mother. Everything." Karen wanted to crawl into one of the lockers and hide from the world.

Dawn's blue eyes were round with sympathy. "Listen, Karen, I know how hard it's been since . . . well, since the other day. People love to gossip and they don't care who they hurt in the process. Tim says this will die a natural death. Everything does, eventually."

"You talked about me to Tim Gilbert?"

"Well, he is my cousin. And he's just wonderful, Karen, he really is. Since I moved to Chrystal Falls, he's been my guardian angel. I can tell him things I can't talk to my mother about. Or even Josh." Dawn looked at her closely. "I think you need someone like that. I'm volunteering to be your guardian angel. How about it?"

Karen was reluctant. She was used to dealing with problems herself — kids from milltown learned to be self-reliant at an early age. "Well —"

"It's hard to open up, I know," Dawn assured her. "I don't want to put you on the spot. Suppose I ask you a question and you answer it if you want to. You haven't mentioned your father lately. Is he okay?" She held up a hand. "If I'm being too nosy, just say so."

"You're not too nosy," Karen said. "I appreciate your concern. I've been so defensive the last few weeks, I hardly know how to act when I'm around a real human." She sighed. "Dad isn't okay. He's terribly depressed, Dawn. I've never seen him this way before. It scares me. And if the Chrystals won't let the workers go back to their old jobs . . . I don't know what'll happen to us then."

"The layoff is temporary. We haven't heard otherwise. Try not to jump to conclusions, Karen. I know it's hard when you're in the middle of a crisis. I remember when my father died. . . ." She blinked, then said, "You're still working nights, aren't you? You look awfully tired these days."

"I am tired. But I can't quit. We need the money," Karen replied tonelessly. "Even though it's not much. I wish I could get another job. One that paid more. . . ." She broke off, shocked that she'd revealed Pickett finances to an outsider.

Dawn deftly sidestepped the subject of money. "You *are* working too hard, Karen. I bet you and Mitch haven't been out in ages."

"He hates the fact I'm working. If I complain about my feet hurting or having too much homework, he always says I should quit and then we have an argument. When it rains it pours," she added, with a wry grin.

Dawn shook her head in admiration. "I can't imagine how you cope with so much responsibility. I flake out if Mom asks me to wipe the dishes two nights in a row."

Karen laughed, but she knew Dawn better than that. "I'm glad you cut assembly. I guess I did need to talk to somebody, but I just didn't realize it. Lately, I have trouble seeing the forest for the trees."

"I'm always around if you need to bend an ear. Give me a call. Or better yet, I'll come over."

Karen returned the admiring glance. "You would, too. You must be the only person on the Hill who's not scared to death to come to my side of town."

"Don't be absurd, Karen. What's the difference between where you live and where, say, Chelsea lives?"

"About five hundred thousand dollars. Surely you've been in Chrystal Falls long enough to see minor differences like that." Karen's tone suddenly hardened.

"I wasn't comparing house styles. I'm talking about the road. The same road that takes me to Chelsea's house goes to your house, more or less. I feel just as free to drive my car up to Chelsea's or down the road to yours."

"Down the road is right," Karen remarked. "You build a pretty convincing case . . . in words. In reality, that road you're talking about ends somewhere around your place. Where it picks up to go to milltown it's bumpy and full of potholes. Or haven't you noticed?"

Now Dawn sighed. "You milltowners are impossible — you just won't see reason. You're as bad as Pete. I can't talk to him either."

"Pete Carter?" Karen was surprised. "He told me that you both called it quits. And when Pete says it's over — whammo, that's it. He's gone in a puff of smoke."

"He was," Dawn confessed, somewhat shyly. "But he reappeared. We've been seeing each other again. He doesn't want anyone to know . . . but you're okay . . . you're milltown." Dawn smiled.

Dawn and Pete together? "That's great, Dawn. He likes you a lot."

"I like him, too, Karen. More than anybody I've ever known."

For a moment Karen forgot her own problems as the full measure of Dawn's words registered. Dawn was in love. "Pete Carter is a very lucky guy," she said softly. "He needs you, Dawn."

"I don't know . . . I wish I could believe that. He runs hot and cold. First we were going out, then we weren't. Now we're seeing each other again. But for how long? I just don't understand —"

Perky and Hollis came into the locker room, laughing over some private joke. Hollis went to her locker and began twirling the combination lock, but Perky went over to join Dawn and Karen.

"My, don't you two look serious. A tête-à-tête? Don't tell me, let me guess. Karen, you were giving Dawn pointers on how to trap a milltown boy, am I right?" Karen observed how well Perky's Arctic smile went with those glacial blue eyes. "Or is it the other way around? Maybe Dawn wants to know how to go after a rich boy just in case she moves to milltown. Karen ought to know all about that. What is it they say? Like mother like daughter?"

Karen was on her feet with the speed and grace of a tigress. "One more crack, Perky Palmer, and you'll be very sorry."

"Are you threatening me?" Perky sounded brave, though she fell back a pace.

Dawn jumped between them. "Stop it, both of you, right now."

"Dawn the peacemaker," Perky sneered.

"How diplomatic were you when you dumped Ian?"

"What's it to you, Palmer?" Karen said. Perky was worse than a snake, always switching loyalties, phony-friendly to whoever was on top at the moment.

Dawn answered instead. "The field is wide open, Perky. Why don't you make your big play for Ian?"

Karen turned away in disgust. "No boy in his right mind would go out with her. Unless she paid him."

Perky opened her mouth to retort but the rest of their class came in then, followed by their P.E. teacher.

Before she went into her glass-walled office, Mrs. Coleman ordered, "All right, girls. No more dilly-dallying. Let's get changed and out on the field."

Chelsea Chrystal wandered into the locker room, looking as if she had stumbled on-stage while an unfamiliar play was in progress. When she saw Dawn, she rushed over.

"Dawn, thank heaven you're here! I need to talk to you! Desperately!" she cried, grabbing Dawn's arm.

Standing a little apart, Karen regarded Chelsea with a critical eye. Despite her expensive outfit, Chelsea didn't look like her normally beautiful self. Today she wore a red buffalo plaid mini-dress that looked like an oversized hunting shirt, belted with black leather. Cable-knit tights continued the bright red theme, and pinned to the cuff of one of

126

her black suede ankle boots was a red c.

No, Karen decided, it wasn't the outfit itself that was less than fantastic. It was Chelsea. The red-and-black cowl collar framing her face robbed the apricot glow from her skin, and stole the sapphire from her eyes. Chelsea looked washed out, like an underdeveloped photograph. Or like someone who hadn't slept in several nights.

Dawn said, "Chelsea, I'm glad to see you, too. Karen and I were just talking . . ." she glanced at Karen, obviously reluctant to reveal the nature of their discussion ". . . about the mill," she fabricated. "Do you have any idea when the layoff will be over?"

Chelsea ran a hand raggedly through her short hair. "Mill? Who cares about the mill! Listen to me, Dawn. I'm in trouble! Someone is after me!"

Dawn's eyes widened. "Chelsea, are you sure?"

"Do I look like I'm lying?" And then Chelsea saw Karen's face. Disbelief was stamped all over it.

"I'll pass on that one," Karen said, her tone laced with spite. "What's the big surprise about somebody being after you? I thought you weren't happy unless you had every male not in rompers in hot pursuit."

"I'm not talking to you," Chelsea told her stiffly. "I was speaking to Dawn. Do you mind leaving us alone?"

Dawn put a hand on Karen's wrist. "No, wait, Karen. Don't go. I'm sorry, Chelsea, but

Karen and I were talking when you came in. She's my friend, too. You can't tell her to leave unless you want me to leave, too."

"All right, stay. I don't care," Chelsea said.

But Karen said, "Dawn, I don't want to hear anything she has to say."

"Stay! Go!" Chelsea nearly shouted. "It doesn't matter to me one way or another. Somebody *listen* to me — I'm in trouble!"

Karen whipped a towel over her shoulder. "What's wrong, Chelsea? Daddy take away your credit cards? You don't know the meaning of trouble." She motioned her head toward the door that led to the fields. The other girls had changed and were already outside, at the gym teacher's coaxing. "I think I'll skip this little discussion. I'm going to play hockey. See you around, Chelsea."

Chelsea clenched Karen's arm in a grip so strong the smaller girl's eyes displayed astonishment. "What did you say?" Chelsea's voice was low and thick, though they were alone in the locker room by now.

"Let go of me!" Karen shook off Chelsea's fingers. "I said I was going outside to play hockey. You got a problem with that?"

"Not that . . . the last thing you said."

Dawn replied quickly, "She said, 'See you around.' Is that what you meant, Chels? Lord, Chelsea, are you going to faint? Karen, get her some water. Quick!"

Room spinning, Chelsea scarcely heard Dawn's directions. She felt strong hands push her shoulders until she was sitting on the bench, then her head was thrust between her knees. She stayed in that position, Dawn's reassuring hand on the back of her neck, until Karen returned with a paper cup of water.

"Can you drink this?" Dawn asked, offering her the cup.

Chelsea sat up and the room fell back into focus. She drank the water. "Thanks. I guess I got a little dizzy just then."

Karen couldn't resist a barb. "How can you tell the difference?" But she was looking at Chelsea carefully.

Dawn frowned at her reprovingly. "Are you sure you're all right, Chelsea? I'll tell Mrs. Coleman you should be excused from practice today. Did you have any breakfast this morning?"

Chelsea rubbed her forehead. "Just a cup of tea. I haven't eaten much lately."

"Worried about a few extra pounds? Honestly, Chelsea, you're slim enough to model umbrella covers now," Karen said.

"She's right," Dawn agreed. "You don't have to diet, Chelsea. Your figure is perfection."

Chelsea felt as if she were going insane. "I haven't eaten not because I'm dieting but because I'm *scared to death*. Haven't you heard a word I've said in the past ten minutes? Somebody is after me!"

Dawn sat down beside her. "*Who* is after you?"

"I don't know! I don't know his name. It's a guy. He calls me on the phone every night."

"Does he say dirty things?" Karen wanted to know. "If he does, you ought to report him to the phone company. They can tell you how to handle him if he calls again."

"He doesn't — they aren't obscene phone calls," Chelsea explained, trying to keep her voice from quavering. "He says things like — well, he always says 'See you around' before he hangs up."

" 'See you around,' " Dawn repeated thoughtfully. "That's what Karen said a few minutes ago. Right before you felt faint."

"And you think I'm behind these calls?" Karen flared. "That tears it, Chrystal. I'm tired of always being blamed for everything."

"I didn't say that. It's a *guy* calling," Chelsea shouted back. "I don't know what to think anymore. But everytime somebody says 'See you around' to me, I think of him. He's out there, waiting to get me."

Karen was obviously not convinced. "Chelsea, stop being so dramatic. You'll try anything for attention. Ever hear the story about the boy who cried wolf? You know what happened to *him*."

"I'm not lying! Why won't anyone believe me? You believe me, don't you, Dawn?" Chelsea appealed to her. "Look, I have proof. This week I started writing down whatever this guy said to me. I have all of his calls recorded, right here in this notebook." She frantically went through the textbooks and notebooks on the bench. The spiral notebook was not among them.

"It's gone!" she whispered incredulously. "My notebook is gone!" Then she remembered the accident in the hall. Those freshman boys who'd run into her, flinging her things to the floor. She doubted the notebook was still in the hall outside the auditorium.

"How convenient," Karen said. "Your notebook has suddenly been stolen. Or did it ever exist in the first place? I think you've been watching too many *Gaslight* reruns on television, Chelsea."

"Wait, Karen," Dawn said. "I don't think Chelsea is making all this up. Not the way she looks." Gently, she spoke to Chelsea. "Don't worry about the notebook. It probably didn't matter that much anyway. Who else have you told about these calls? Your parents?"

"No. My grandparents are in Palm Springs and Mother is out of town for the next few days. And Daddy—" Chelsea broke off to glare at Karen. "I can't talk to my father, anymore, thanks to you!"

"What do *I* have to do with you and your father?" Karen demanded, fists on hips.

"Ever since you told me about my father and—and your mother, I've hardly been able to face him." A shrewd look crossed Chelsea's features. "You don't believe me—why should I believe you? What if I say you're lying about my father? How do I know you aren't making the whole thing up? You and your mother."

Karen narrowed her own eyes. "I didn't even ask my mother about this until your father came in the country club one night. When he saw me, he called me by her name, right in front of *your* mother. *That's* how I know."

Chelsea felt the blood ebb from her face. "He called your mother's name? In the country club?" There was no doubt what Karen said was true. No wonder Elizabeth frowned when Chelsea asked if she had been her father's first love.

"Chelsea," Dawn said, "forget about that. You've got to tell your father. You can't go on indefinitely, letting this guy bother you. Talk to your father tonight."

But Chelsea knew she couldn't. Not now. Not ever. Her father was obviously wrestling with problems of his own. Even if she did approach him, suppose he didn't believe her any more than Karen did? She no longer had the notebook to back her up.

No one can help me, she thought in despair. And that man will never stop until he gets me.

Chapter Eleven

Dawn didn't expect to see him tonight, but he suddenly materialized out of the dense fog like a restless spirit left over from Halloween.

She bit back a scream, even though Abner didn't growl or give his warning bark the way he did when he thought his mistress was in danger. In fact, his tail beat the air as he greeted his old friend.

"Pete! My gosh, you scared me half to death," she gasped. Ordinarily she wouldn't have been so jumpy, but a lot occupied her mind tonight as she walked the dog down to the river. Karen's worries over her parents . . . and Chelsea's startling revelation that someone was after her. She'd been thinking about Chelsea mainly, when the figure stepped out of the drifting mists, blocking her path.

"Sorry," he said, both hands jammed into

the pockets of his jacket. "I didn't mean to frighten you."

"I guess I'm a little jittery tonight," she admitted, passing Abner's leash to Pete so they could stroll along the river bank. "With the fog and everything. Most of the time I'm not afraid to come down here alone, but tonight . . . I've got the willies."

"I wouldn't let anyone lay a hand on you," Pete said fiercely. "You really shouldn't come down here by yourself. That's why I've left work early lately, so I could keep an eye on you."

Dawn was stunned. "You mean, you've been down here waiting for me? How come I haven't seen you?"

"Usually I stand over there, on high ground." He indicated the small bluff where they had flown the dragon kite — the last time they'd been together for several days. "I can see you from up there — and anybody else who comes along. If some bozo ever tried anything, I'd be there in five seconds flat."

Dawn thought this was the most romantic thing she'd ever heard. Watching her from afar to make sure she wasn't bothered. "You still haven't answered my other question. Why did you show up tonight?"

They stopped. Pete unhooked Abner's leash to let the dog run a little and explore the water's edge. There was no one in sight on the path. Heavy curtains of fog enclosed them; the rest of the world ceased to exist beyond the few yards they were able to see.

"Because," he said at last. "You looked so —vulnerable and lonely. And because I couldn't bear to watch you leave me again."

"Leave you?"

He laughed, embarrassed. "I know it sounds dumb, but for a week I've stood up on that bluff and waited for you. I'd pretend that you were coming to see me and that we'd go off someplace together. But all that ever happened was you'd walk Abner a little while and then you'd turn around and go home. It was like you were leaving me."

"Pete, if I'd known —" The time they'd wasted! The hours she'd sat at home or in class, enduring the pain of his absence.

"Forget it," he said brusquely. "I told you it was stupid. It's my own fault, staying away from you. God, Dawn, do you know how many nights I couldn't sleep because of you? Seeing your eyes, remembering how silky your hair feels. . . ." He paused, as if he wanted to touch her hair again, to prove to himself she was real. "I keep trying to figure out how we can make it work. But the facts don't change. You're from up here . . . and I'm from down there. I hate all this deceit. You're too good for that."

Dawn said nothing. Instead she avoided Pete's face, letting her eyes wander down the bank to the water, where Abner was snuffling an old Big Mac container. Weekend rains had swelled Rapid River and the current, living up to its name, rushed downstream swiftly, as if it had an appointment to keep. How many times had she and Pete stood near this very spot, either talking like the best of friends, or standing yards apart without acknowledging the other's presence.

She recalled the words of a writer she'd read. He used a river as a metaphor for the impermanence of one's life, maintaining that it was impossible to visit the same river twice — each time the onlooker returned to the river, he was a different person, just as the river was always changing.

Are we different people whenever we come here? Dawn wondered now. She and Pete always seemed to be at a different place in their lives, even from one day to the next. And yet they were pulled back here, time and again. Ten minutes, one minute, whatever they could steal from a world that pried them apart. She loved him and needed to see him. Had to see him. Just as she had to breathe, in order to stay alive.

He felt the same.

She turned to look at him. A lock of fog-dampened hair fell over his forehead. Under the muffled glow of the streetlamp, she saw undisguised longing in his eyes, raw, poignant. For the first time, Dawn was absolutely certain Pete Carter loved her.

And then his lips came down on hers, so quickly it was as if he didn't want her to see that look anymore, as if he regretted showing his feelings too much. Dawn sank into the kiss, twining her arms around his neck, hearing only the sound of the river lapping the shore. Their differences fell away like ice thawing under the spring sun. The mill toppled to the ground and the mansions up on the hill slid into a harmless heap. They were simply a boy and a girl who loved each other, and nothing else mattered.

When they separated reluctantly, Pete whispered into her hair, "What are we going to do, Newhouse?"

"I don't know," was the only answer she could give. She didn't want to think about the future, the next hour even. It was enough being in his arms, knowing that he loved her. If only she could fast-freeze this moment, turn it into a still photograph. She would take Pete's hand and step into the enchanted place they had made, leaving Chrystal Falls behind forever.

Stark reality in the form of a very wet dog brought her abruptly down to earth. "Abner!" she scolded as he offered her a soggy paw. "You're filthy! Get off me!"

Pete laughed, and the river seemed to vibrate with the rich sound. Someone should bottle that laugh, Dawn thought, and send a jar to every sad or oppressed person in the world.

"Great timing," he said to Abner, gently pushing the dog away from Dawn so he could attach his leash to his collar. "About as good as mine."

Dawn would not let him spoil their special mood. "Your timing is perfect. I told you this a long time ago, but you keep forgetting. I'll always be here for you, Pete. I love you."

She understood his difficulty verbalizing his innermost feelings, as if he feared rebuff or condemnation the minute intimate words left his mouth. But before he kissed her again, he said, "I love you, too," in a whisper so slight Dawn wasn't sure she hadn't imagined it.

The fog drew protective wings around them, and the river swept past, hurrying on.

Pete swung the "pages" of the jukebox selections one more time, dropped a quarter in the slot at the top, then pushed a couple of buttons. After a momentary pause, the strains of Barbra Streisand's "The Way We Were" poured from the instrument, sweet and heart-rending.

"You chose that?" Dawn said, surprised. "I never knew you were so sentimental."

"There's a lot of things you don't know about me," he returned. "That song reminds me of us."

"But it's such a sad song. And it's about a romance that ended. Is that the way you think of us? In the past tense?" Dawn felt no hesitation asking Pete these questions. They had met at the river for the last three nights, where they talked, and tried to iron out their problems. She believed their relationship was on much stronger footing now. When he asked if she wanted to go out again, she accepted readily, reinforcing her promise that she was always willing to meet him halfway.

"Should I tell my mother who I'm going out with?" Dawn had asked hopefully. How long would they continue to meet secretly?

Pete's features tightened and Dawn was afraid he'd call off the whole thing. But he only replied, "Not yet."

He took her to a coffee shop not too far from where he worked, on the fringe of mill-town before it evolved into the Strip. Not Mom and Pop's, but still nice. A group of tiny tables crowded the long, narrow room, but Pete led Dawn to a booth in the very back.

As the song came to its plaintive finish, Pete reached out for Dawn's hands, a gesture that made her heart sing. They sat this way, hands clasped on the formica-covered table, until a waitress brought their menus. Dawn leaned back in the booth, the vinyl cushion crackling beneath her shoulder blades, and studied the handwritten choices.

"Four-Alarm Chili!" she cried. "Pete, don't you know any place that serves regular food?"

He took her menu away and set it aside with his. "You haven't lived until you've had the chili here."

"I may not live *after* I've had the chili here," she amended dryly. "Do they bring plenty of water? Is there a fire extinguisher handy?"

"I can see you need to be introduced to the fine art of eating chili. For one thing, drinking water only makes the fire hotter. Eat bread instead." Winking at her, he said in a Texas drawl, "Why, Miss, eating Sadie's chili is practically a test of manhood around these parts. Only the fittest survive."

"Test of manhood, huh? Wonder how I'll do?" Dawn thought longingly of reducing her order to a bowl of mere Two-Alarm Chili, but realized there was more at stake here than a flaming stomach. If Pete thought she could stand it, she wouldn't disappoint him.

When the thick pottery dishes arrived, piled to the rim with thick chunks of beef so peppery-looking she half-expected them to snarl at her, Dawn exclaimed, "No beans! Who ever heard of chili without beans?"

Pete flashed her a withering glance. "Real chili, for you novices, does not have beans. In the old days, the trail cooks only used beans when they were running out of meat, to make the pot go farther."

"Pardon me," she said with exaggerated politeness. "I had no idea I was dining in the presence of a chili purist." Bravely she lifted a spoonful to her mouth, sent a silent prayer heavenward, then ate it. It really wasn't so bad, once she got used to each bite burning a fiery trail down her throat.

They had finished dinner and were arguing amiably about what to have for dessert, when Pete suddenly froze.

"What is it?" Dawn had her back to the rest of the room and couldn't see without leaning out of the booth. "Is it somebody we know?"

"Karen's mother," he reported in a low voice. "And . . . if I'm not mistaken, that's Mr. Chrystal. Chelsea's father."

Dawn spun around in the booth. Pete was right. She recognized the small, dark-haired woman as Gloria Pickett. Her pretty features were blurred with unhappiness, her cheeks as pale as faded primrose petals.

The gentleman behind her was indeed Chelsea's father, distinguished as ever in a Burberry trenchcoat. He was hatless and his silvering hair shone in the florescent lighting. He led Mrs. Pickett to an empty table near their booth.

Dawn couldn't tear her eyes away from the couple, as Alexander Chrystal helped Gloria take off her coat. They both darted wary glances around the restaurant, as if they were nervous about being seen together, but they did not look over to where Dawn and Pete sat in the far booth. The waitress brought them each coffee, but the cups remained untouched at their elbows, they were so engrossed in their conversation.

Pete snatched the check and stood up, throwing a bill on the table. "Let's get out of here."

"Why? We shouldn't let those people ruin our evening," Dawn protested. "And anyway they aren't bothering us."

141

"Well, they're bothering me! Don't you know who they are? And what they're doing?"

"They'll hear you, Pete. They look to me like they're talking. What's the big crime in that?"

"The big crime is, they're ruining their lives and everybody else's."

"Doing what? Having a cup of coffee?" She couldn't believe Pete was making such a big deal out of something so trivial.

"You know perfectly well what I'm talking about. They're sneaking around, meeting in places a Chrystal would never go to."

"For heaven's sake, Pete. They'd hardly meet in a place this public if they didn't want to be seen. You're as bad as the kids at school, spreading rumors," Dawn said heatedly. "That's how people get hurt. Karen Pickett has been miserable for weeks because of this. Chelsea, too."

"Let me tell you something, Dawn. Karen is miserable because she found out about her mother and that — that pompous idiot over there. He pretended to love her once and then he dumped her because she wasn't good enough. That's what happens when Hill and Mill tangle, Dawn. It never works out. There's living proof."

"What are you saying?" Now she was angry. "That I'm pretending to love you and then I'll dump you? Pete, no matter what I do or say, it doesn't seem to make any *difference* to you. You only believe what you want to be-lieve." Then the truth jolted her like an electric current. "It's not this Hill and Mill thing that's upsetting you at all. It's because you think they're meeting secretly, isn't it? Just like we are."

But he was already at the counter, paying the check. Dawn slid from the booth, plucking her coat from the hook on the divider. She glanced over at Mrs. Pickett and Mr. Chrystal. Their conversation was low and guarded, their expressions reflecting a distant sadness, as though they had gone back to the river and found that too much water had flowed past for them to find their way back to their enchanted place.

Taking a quarter from her bag, Dawn dropped it into the jukebox. She pushed the selection buttons. "The Way We Were" began to play once more.

At the door, Pete was talking urgently to someone. Dawn caught up with him and saw he was trying to keep Karen Pickett from entering the restaurant.

"Go home, Karen," he urged, half-pushing her back out the door.

"Will you stop! What's the matter with you, Pete Carter? Are you crazy?" Ducking under his arm, Karen shoved past Dawn and into the dining room. She moaned softly as she saw her mother with Alexander Chrystal. "Not again."

"It could be nothing," Dawn hastened to reassure her. "After all, lots of people go to restaurants. They're just talking."

Karen looked at her for the first time and

Dawn felt herself shriveling under a gaze hotter than any Four-Alarm Chili.

"It's none of your business, Dawn, what they're doing."

"Karen!"

"You don't belong here," Karen said. "You never have and you never will."

"I'm only trying to help. I'm your friend, Karen." Dawn felt as if she'd been stung.

"We'll solve our problems ourselves like we always have."

As Karen went over to stand beside Pete, Dawn took one look at his closed, immobile face and knew she had lost him again.

They left the coffee shop with the final haunting melody of "The Way We Were" echoing in her ears.

Dawn wished for the comfort of the river, but the stream was blocks away. She had to deal with this new situation in the unyielding armor of Pete's car, parked in front of her apartment building.

"Pete," she began. "I'm sorry. I didn't mean to compare us to Mr. Chrystal and Mrs. Pickett."

Pete sat rigidly behind the steering wheel. "Forget it. They were sneaking around, we've been sneaking around. There's no way to color it any differently."

"Then let's stop making excuses. We'll go out tomorrow night. Or any night you name. You can come in and meet my mother. We'll make it official. Please!"

"It won't —"

"Don't say it won't work," she pleaded. "I don't care what other people think. I only care for you. And I know you care for me."

Light from the streetlamp poured in through the car window at an angle, isolating Dawn in a silvery pool, but leaving Pete in a pocket of darkness.

"Give me time," was all he said.

Dawn grasped at that cobwebby filament of hope as though it were a rope woven of steel. She would wait forever, if she had to.

Chapter Twelve

Chelsea's descent into uncharacteristic deception had begun with a phone call that afternoon when she got home from school. Not from *him* — it was too early — but her mother. Elizabeth had decided to stay on in Philadelphia one more night. That way, she explained, she could wait for the Judge's and Grandmother Lillian's flight from Palm Springs, so they wouldn't have to take that dreary connecting flight into Chrystal Falls. They would all arrive home in plenty of time before Thanksgiving, Elizabeth reassured her daughter.

"Do you have to stay?" Chelsea had cried. "Can't you come home tonight? Daddy can drive you into Philadelphia tomorrow afternoon to pick up Grandmother and the Judge."

"Chelsea, do you hear yourself? My dear,

you're not making one bit of sense. Your father has court tomorrow; he can't go traipsing off to Philadelphia. I'm already here — why should I come home? Give Amy a big kiss for me, love. I'll see you both tomorrow night."

That might be too late, Chelsea thought, putting the receiver in its cradle. She stared at the phone, half-expecting it to ring again. He was going to call tonight. She knew that as well as she knew her own name. She felt the game was almost over — sensed the caller was tired of stringing her along. Soon he would make his move.

The house was empty just then. Marie was downtown, buying groceries for the Thanksgiving feast day after tomorrow. Amy was out riding with her friend Maggie Janko. And her father was still at work.

Suppose *he* knew she was all alone. What if he was just outside her window, waiting. . . .

Chelsea couldn't tear her eyes away from the phone on her night table. She had become a prisoner of the white plastic instrument, a slave to it. Any second now she'd be summoned by the shrill ringing.

She seized the receiver and, with trembling fingers, dialed Dawn's number, but Josh answered.

"Oh, hi, Chelsea. Dawn's not here right now," he said, sounding so sane and normal she almost sobbed with relief.

"Oh, that's too bad." Of course, Dr. Newhouse was at the hospital. Josh Newhouse, tennis star and all-around hunk, was as alone as she was. On impulse, Chelsea skillfully maneuvered the conversation from tennis and school chit-chat to the tantalizing suggestion of taking a lonely but dazzling girl out dancing. Before he could think about it, Josh had agreed to take her dancing at the Yellow Brick Road later that night.

But then Josh asked her two questions, prompting the white lies. He wondered how often she'd been to this disco, to which she replied, "Zillions of times." Still unsure, Josh then asked if she had permission to go to a place like that on a school night. Implying that her father would let her fly the Concorde to Paris for breakfast if she wanted, Chelsea airily brushed away Josh's concerns.

Her father. He was part of the reason she had to get out tonight. If she could only go to him, tell him about her tormentor . . . but that was impossible. Alexander Chrystal wasn't someone she trusted anymore.

The hard driving beat of rock music thundered around them the instant they stepped into the disco.

Josh Newhouse pulled at his jacket as a group of people squeezed by him, nearly taking his coat with them. "Are you sure you want to go to this place?" he asked Chelsea, his tone skeptical.

"Of course. I come here all the time." Taking him by the hand, Chelsea dragged him into the pulsing mob, gyrating under the arch of a green neon rainbow.

She had told two lies to get Josh to take her to the Yellow Brick Road tonight. But they were only tiny white lies and, anyway, who cared what she did these days?

She was absolutely forbidden to go to the Yellow Brick Road, a club located just outside Chrystal Falls that attracted a rougher, older crowd. From the street, Yellow Brick Road appeared pretty nondescript — housed in an old warehouse with only a small sign over the plain wooden door. But inside, the club was decorated in early MGM. A simulated yellow brick tile road spiraled from the entranceway to the raised dance floor. Green neon arrows pointed toward the "Emerald City," a smoke-clouded dais where a bored-looking drummer pounded drums in time to the taped music. Stills of Judy Garland and the other actors from *The Wizard of Oz* movie were framed in chrome and hung along the green-painted walls.

Edging the dance platform, Munchkin-sized tables crowded together like toadstools sprouting in a neon-green forest. Chelsea led Josh to an empty table and they sat down. A girl wearing a green tee-shirt that read "Toto, I Don't Think We're In Kansas Anymore" offered to take their drink orders.

"Cokes," Josh said quickly. "Right?"

"A Coke is fine," Chelsea told him. "Just

because they serve the hard stuff here, doesn't mean that's what I want to drink. Anyway, I came here to have a good time. And that's what we're going to do." She leaned back in her chair. She needed this place tonight. Definitely.

"You look terrific," Josh said. "Prettiest girl here."

Chelsea laughed delightedly. "That's not saying much, Josh Newhouse. Have you looked around?"

He grinned back. "Yeah. There are a lot of weirdos. Most of the girls out on that dance floor look like refugees from an off-beat music video."

Chelsea knew she looked great. Her outfit was part of her strategy — if she wanted to knock over Josh Newhouse, she had to bring out the big guns. Over black satin tapered pants, she wore a loose ivory and black satin blouse, the low sash caught at one hip with a rhinestone buckle. Because Josh was wonderfully tall, she wore black sandals with skyscraper heels. A bracelet of chunky crystals like ice cubes, her signature jewelry, encircled her wrist, catching the light from the revolving mirrored ball overhead and throwing it back in glittery splinters.

"I'm really surprised you called this afternoon," Josh was saying.

"Just surprised? Not thrilled?" Chelsea said, teasing him.

"That, too. Still, I thought you were Ryan

Simpson's territory. That's why I've stayed away."

Chelsea lifted her chin slightly. "I'm *no one's* territory. If anything, Ryan's *my* territory. Really, Josh, we just go around together. He's good for a laugh now and then." She flicked him a smoldering glance through her lashes. "Since you brought it up, are you looking for a claim to stake, Josh Newhouse?"

He ducked his head to sip his Coke, as if suddenly uncomfortable. Chelsea loved it. He *was* interested — anyone within a fifty-mile radius could pick up his signals.

When he looked at her again, his eyes were questioning.

"What?" she asked, sensitive to his every mood.

"I'm not sure exactly. You seem . . . different than you usually are."

Any other girl would have pressed for clarification at this moment: "Different? How?" But she wanted him to observe her more, absorb this bewitching, grown-up Chelsea, without shattering the image by asking juvenile questions. Interesting a man was an extremely delicate operation to Chelsea, requiring carefully doled-out information, tempered by enough mystery to keep the boy in a state of perpetual fascination.

She sat back, pretending to watch the dancers slinging themselves around on the dance platform.

The music changed to one of Chelsea's

favorite songs. "Let's dance," she said, grabbing Josh's hand. They threaded their way through the jostling throng on the platform, clearing a sliver of floor space for themselves.

Josh was an excellent dancer. He moved as well on the dance floor as he did on the tennis court, following her movements with an athlete's precision.

Conversation was impossible, but that didn't bother Chelsea. She used her arms, her legs, her hips to convey how she felt about him. She let her eyes say things to him she'd never have the nerve to say aloud. Was he responding by matching her steps, letting her know he felt the same about her? It was difficult to tell in such a crush.

"It's pretty hot in here!" Josh exclaimed when the song crashed to an end and another spun from the stereo speakers mounted overhead. "Can we go outdoors a minute?"

"I want to dance some more," Chelsea said. "I thought we were going to have fun."

"We are having fun," Josh yelled over the music. "I just need some air, that's all. Besides, it's getting pretty late."

"No, it isn't. We just *got* here," she protested. "One more dance and then we'll sit the next one out."

A young man wearing tight jeans and a black sweat shirt moved between them, whirling Chelsea around. "I'll dance with you, baby. Send Junior home if you want." He nodded toward Josh.

"Let me go!" Chelsea yanked her arm free with anger. No one touched Chelsea Chrystal unless she wanted to be touched. Who *was* this guy? Could he be the man making the calls? Suddenly the nightmare that had consumed her life for the past few weeks reared up like the Loch Ness monster, filling her with dread and raising a terrifying possibility. So many people — any *one* of them could be The Caller. They were all so close, bumping her, touching her as they danced —

"Come on, honey. I'll show you a real good time." The stranger was persistent, reaching out for her again.

Chelsea was nearly incoherent with fear. "I-I don't want to dance. Leave me alone! Josh!"

"You heard the lady," Josh told the man evenly. "She doesn't want to dance with you." In the flashing lights, his blue eyes darkened to a dangerous cobalt. "I think we'd better go home now, Chelsea."

In the car, she slumped into the seat. Before Josh started the engine, he stared at her. This time Chelsea didn't bother to act mysterious. She looked into his eyes, bundled to the chin in her fur jacket.

"It's funny," he said after a while. "I used to dream about what it would be like to take you out, Chelsea." He laughed shortly. "I suppose that's the fantasy of every male in Chrystal Falls High."

Her heart turned over, despite the awful fear she'd just experienced.

"And now that we've gone out, I'm not sure what happened." He shook his head. "This wasn't the kind of date I expected. You're not the *girl* I expected. You seem to be, well — sort of at different levels. I don't think you really had a good time. Why did you ask me to take you to this place?" He backed the car out of the parking lot.

For once, Chelsea had no ready reply. She was drained. The evening hadn't gone the way she planned either. Josh didn't really care for her after all. No one did. Not her mother, or else she would have heard the plea in her daughter's voice and come right home. Not her father, who had other matters on his mind these days, such as Karen Pickett's mother. Not Ryan — he thought she was taking the strange phone calls too seriously. She had futilely hoped Josh would come to her rescue, but she hadn't known what to ask for.

She doubted Josh Newhouse would ever want to go out with her again. He had better things to do than complicate his life.

Chelsea pressed her cheek against the window, tilting her head back to search the night sky. The stars were out in sparkling abundance, brittle chips of crystal. When she was very young, she used to think her father had flung the stars up into the sky with a lavish hand, just for her. She could always count on the stars — they belonged to her. Now she knew the stars weren't made of crystal, naturally, nor had they been tossed up there by her father. She couldn't count on the stars anymore. Or her father.

Josh drove her home, tactfully playing easy rock on the radio to mask the fact that neither of them felt much like talking.

"I don't suppose you want to come in," Chelsea said.

"Thanks, but it's late."

"Well. Good-night, then."

"Chelsea." He spoke her name as though it were an enigma, something marvelous yet unattainable.

His hand brushed her cheek, soft as a butterfly wing, then went around her neck to pull her into a kiss. Josh's lips on hers were anything but tentative. Chelsea gave herself completely to his embrace, giddy from the intensity of his ardor, and thrilled that, for once, a man had taken the initiative, made a move she hadn't orchestrated.

Then he released her, as suddenly as he'd kissed her. "Good-night, Chelsea."

" 'Night, Josh. Thanks for being with me tonight." Perhaps all isn't lost, Chelsea thought, letting herself in the front door.

The house was quiet, though it wasn't that late. The faint strains of the *MASH* theme told her Amy was watching television. A sword of light from under her father's study door slashed the dim hall. He was home, apparently unconcerned that she had gone out.

155

She guessed he had believed the excuse she gave Amy, that she was going to the country club for dinner. If he learned she'd been to the Yellow Brick Road, he wouldn't be working so diligently in his den. Or would he? Did she really know her father? How could a man with a wife as beautiful and charming as Elizabeth even think about another woman?

Kicking off her high heels, Chelsea sprawled across her bed. The phone rang.

She froze.

It was him.

Much as she wanted, she couldn't grab the phone and wrench it from the wall. Something compelled her to answer it.

She picked up the receiver and listened, instead of saying hello.

"It's me, Chels," the horribly familiar voice breathed into her ear. "Did you think I forgot you? No way. Have a nice time at Yellow Brick Road? Can't say much for your new boyfriend, though. He looked like a dud."

Her heart thudded. He knew where she went tonight! He must have followed her! Or maybe he had been there.

"Listen to me," she said, spacing her words so he wouldn't hear how scared she was. "This is the last time you're calling me. Tomorrow I'm having the phone taken out so you won't be able —"

"Oh, don't bother, Chels. After tomorrow it won't matter whether you have a phone or not."

Her knees turned to water. Oh, my God — he really was after her! "Wh-what do you mean?"

"This is the last time I'm calling you. The very last time." His voice softened to a satisfied whisper that chilled Chelsea.

"Why are you doing this to me? I've never done anything to you. I don't even know who you are!"

"You'll find out soon enough. And you've done plenty to me. You and your family has. The rich Chrystals — hire 'em and fire 'em, just so long as nothing interferes with their parties."

"What are you talking about?"

"You don't have any idea, do you? And why should you? You have everything you could possibly want. Your daddy's rich. Your granddaddy practically owns the town. What do you care if half the people in milltown are out of work?"

That mill again! He must be one of the employees laid off a few weeks ago, like Karen's father. That was around the time she began getting the phone calls, her mind calculated frantically. Karen's father was included in that cutback. Was *he* her caller? This man sounded younger than she expected Karen's father to be, but voices *could* be altered.

"So you see, Chels," he went on, his tone shifting into a higher, more menacing register, "*somebody* has to teach you a lesson. To make sure you understand just how hard it is on the other side of the fence."

"Oh, I understand perfectly! If you'll just give me your name, I can talk to my father and you'll have your job back by tomorrow morning! I promise!" Chelsea pleaded with tears running down her cheeks.

He laughed. "Nice try, but you're too late. Bye-bye, Chels. Be seeing you around."

Click.

He was gone.

But not for long. This time she knew he would keep his parting promise.

Chapter Thirteen

"Where's Dad?" Karen asked, feeling a momentary stab of panic as she walked into the living room. Her father wasn't sitting in his usual chair, watching television.

"Out working," Johnny replied. He was playing Solitaire on the coffee table. "Got a job winterizing some houses over in your friend Dawn's neighborhood. You know, cleaning out gutters, fixing downspouts, stuff like that. Same thing he did around here last week."

"Really? That's great." Karen tossed her school books on the sofa and sat down, relieved that her father hadn't done something drastic.

For the past month, Carl Pickett had wandered around the house like the last survivor of a plane crash, talking only when spoken to. Saturday, Karen's mother begged him to clean the leaves clogging the gutters and do other minor repairs around the house. When Carl came inside later that afternoon, his cheeks ruddy from the brisk air, he cheerfully announced he planned to go from house to house, offering his services as a handyman.

"Everybody hates getting ready for winter," he said to his wife, washing his hands at the sink. "So next week I'm going around town and see if anybody wants me to put in their storm windows, nail down loose shingles, whatever." He chuckled. "A lot of men would rather watch football Thanksgiving than worry about downspouts."

After his initial fruitless attempts to get a job, this was Carl's first real step toward regaining his role as head of the family. Karen still didn't approve of the way he refused to let her mother get a job, but at least he was trying, not vegetating in front of the TV or languishing over the sports page of the newspaper.

"You off tonight?" Johnny asked Karen, placing a red jack on a red queen. Only Johnny cheated unselfconsciously at solitaire.

"Yeah, but I have to work Thanksgiving. In the main dining room, too. My boss told me that's one of the country club's busiest days. So I have off tonight and tomorrow night."

"Lucky you," Johnny said. "I have to work every night and Thursday, too."

Karen picked at a chipped thumbnail. "You think Mom will be mad? Because we won't be here Thanksgiving?"

160

Johnny shook his head. "I already told her I had to work. She didn't get upset. At least it's a few bucks more this week."

"We've always been together on Thanksgiving," Karen said. "This will be the first year —"

"It's only a day." Johnny waved the king of diamonds. But Karen knew her brother minded as much as she did, despite his breezy lack of concern. Unable to find a place for his king, he tossed it on the table in disgust. "Want to play Hearts or something?"

She stared at the intricate design on the back of Johnny's card, remembering how she used to trace the pattern with one finger, seeking a way out of the maze. "No. I wish Mom would buy a new deck of cards. That one is about a hundred years old." She got up abruptly and went into the kitchen.

Gloria Pickett was at the table, clipping coupons from Sunday's paper. "Hello, Karen. I didn't hear you come in."

"Hi." She scarcely acknowledged her mother, busying herself with getting the peanut butter and crackers from the cupboard. Her mother didn't know that Karen had seen her with Chelsea's father in the coffee shop. It wasn't the kind of thing she could mention over crackers and milk, accuse her own mother of having a love affair with another man.

"Anything happen in school today?"

"No," Karen mumbled. Unless you counted the snide remarks some kids made when she walked by. Dawn's cousin Tim was wrong.

He claimed the gossip about Gloria and Alexander would die a natural death, but rumors were still rushing unimpeded throughout the school, with the force of a flood.

"You're awfully quiet," her mother observed, putting her scissors down and gathering her pile of coupons. "Are you getting enough sleep? I wish you didn't work so late on school nights. It's not good for you."

"I'm fine. As a matter of fact, I'm off tonight and tomorrow night both. But I have to work Thanksgiving."

"So does Johnny," Gloria sighed. "Oh, well, I'll have dinner later than usual, so we can all be together. It isn't right for families to be apart on Thanksgiving."

Karen felt a lump in her throat and wasn't sure it was the peanut butter cracker she'd just swallowed. How could her mother rattle on about families being together on Thanksgiving, when she was seeing Alexander Chrystal behind her husband's back?

"What time will Dad be home?" she asked. Maybe if she kept bringing her father into the conversation, her mother might start feeling guilty.

Gloria glanced at the clock. "About six or a little after. Karen, he was like a new man when he walked out the door this morning. It means the world to him to be working again, doing anything, just so he's earning money."

Karen wondered how her mother could speak of her father, after what she'd done.

"Maybe now he won't act like he hates Johnny and me for getting jobs at the country club."

"Don't say that!" Her mother's normally gentle voice was vehement. "Your father has *never* hated you or Johnny, no matter what either of you did. Sure, he was upset when you both went to work — it's a hard thing to face when a man loses his job and his children have to bring in the paychecks. But he's getting used to it, just as we've all learned to adjust. Look at the way he argues with Johnny — that's his way of showing how much he cares about the boy. If he didn't, he'd let Johnny run wild. But Carl is tough on his son because he's afraid of what might happen to him. He wants both you kids to know right from wrong. He loves us, Karen. Don't you ever forget it."

"Do *you* still love Daddy?" Karen said before she realized the words had left her lips.

Her mother seemed genuinely shocked. "Why on earth would you ask a thing like that? Of course, I love your father. Why shouldn't I?"

"Well, he's not exactly been himself since the layoff." Karen wanted her mother to confess her clandestine meeting with Alexander Chrystal, get it out in the open.

"Karen, just because your father is unemployed, doesn't mean I gave up on him, gave up on our marriage. We work through these times, until we're over the rough spots. Carl will either get called back to the mill or he'll find other work. Either way we'll manage. Our lives are far from over. This is only a temporary setback."

Her mother sounded sincere, but Karen still couldn't shake the queasy feeling of betrayal. She had seen her mother with Mr. Chrystal the other night. They looked very intimate. There was no denying it.

Johnny came into the kitchen then, riffling the deck of cards with the dexterity of a Las Vegas blackjack dealer. "I'm bored," he declared. "Anybody want to play cards?"

"I told you once, no," Karen replied, irritated. How could her brother act so silly when their parents' marriage was in trouble? "Why aren't you out fooling around with your buddies?" she said shortly.

"Me? What about you? You aren't exactly Miss Congeniality yourself," he countered. "What happened to that pretty blackhaired girl, Dawn? She never comes over anymore."

"She told me she had errands to run after school today," Karen hedged, trying to forget the fact that Dawn and Pete had also seen Gloria and Alexander in the coffee shop. Pete she could trust — he was a milltowner, after all — but Dawn . . . she just didn't know.

"Besides," she added tartly, "Dawn hangs around Chelsea Chrystal too much. And you know how I feel about the Chrystals. I loathe them all."

"Karen!" her mother said angrily. "What is the matter with you this evening? That remark was uncalled for."

"If it weren't for them, we'd all be together Thanksgiving and Dad wouldn't be out cleaning gutters."

"There's nothing wrong with what your father is doing," she told Karen. "We're managing just fine."

"But the Chrystals get away scot-free," Karen insisted. "They have everything."

"Not everything," Gloria argued. "Their world is not as perfect as you think."

Karen stared at her mother, almost forgetting to breathe. "How would you know?"

"I once glimpsed life on the Hill. It wasn't for me."

"Not then," Karen allowed. "But what about now? Wouldn't you rather live like Mrs. Chrystal, without worries? Have plenty of money?"

"I don't know what's gotten into you," Gloria rebuffed. She pulled out a chair for Johnny, who was lounging against the refrigerator. "Come on. I'll play cards with you."

"Don't mind Karen." He sat down and began shuffling the deck. "She's bent out of shape because she has to work Thursday."

"Is that why, Karen?" her mother asked.

She shrugged, sick with misery. She wanted Mitch, suddenly. He was the only person in the whole world she could rely on completely. She hadn't seen him since the day when they had stopped at the coffee shop. He had been parking the car and she had gone inside to get a table . . . and then she'd seen her mother in deep discussion with Alexander Chrystal.

165

Her eyes filled with tears. Where would it all end?

Johnny said, "These are pretty old cards, Mom. I don't know if they'll last the game. Why don't you buy some new ones?"

Gloria fingered the rounded edges of the deck, so worn from use that the paper had split into soft dog-ears. "I imagine they'll last quite a while longer," she mused. "Join us, Karen?"

"Come on, bubble-gum face," Johnny urged, lapsing into the hateful name he tagged her with ages ago. "I'll even let you win."

Karen shook her head. Johnny didn't know what she knew. He thought the affair with Chelsea's father was past history, but it was still going on. She couldn't sit there at the kitchen table, blithely playing Hearts with the deck of souvenir cards brought back from her parents' honeymoon trip to the Great Smoky Mountains.

"I've got studying to do," she muttered, and stalked into her room.

Along the Strip, storefronts were dark and shuttered, stiffly facing the street with blind windows as if forcing winter to grope its way into town. Buffeted by a sharp wind, steel-wool clouds rasped against a thin, defenseless moon. In November, dusk descended all at once, settling down like wet newspapers and blending into night with a blackness that was so absolute and final Karen wondered if daylight would ever come again. Street lamps placed at intervals along the curb did their best to scrape back some of the night, their weak beams illuminating the sidewalk with translucent puddles.

Karen jogged down "A" Avenue, her feet hitting the pavement, silently mulling over a mixture of thoughts. In spite of the cold and gloom, it felt good to exercise outdoors, something she had missed since she began working at the country club.

Her father had come home at six in high spirits, giving his wife a big kiss, praising the ordinary Tuesday-night meat loaf as if it were saddle of lamb. It was like the old days, before the layoff.

Karen watched her parents during supper. She noticed the little exchanges that went on between them — a lift of the eyebrows, a secret smile, a private joke that neither she nor Johnny had understood. Maybe that was the key to her parents' marriage. They had a past — years shared before she and Johnny ever arrived on the scene. That was what her mother tried to tell her earlier — you didn't throw away a lifetime of love because your husband was unemployed. You worked through the rough times.

Yet how could she account for what she had seen in the coffee shop? If her mother loved her father so much, why would she risk her marriage for a few stolen minutes with Alexander Chrystal?

The answer eluded her. She needed help sorting it out. Mitch. She had to talk to Mitch.

Karen quickened her step past the dry cleaners and the used book store. There was a phone booth on the corner. She'd call Mitch at the garage and ask him to take a break and come get her. They could drive to their special spot overlooking the river and talk. The thought of Mitch's understanding brown eyes and the warmth of his arms around her renewed her love for him in a single sweet burst like the flare of a Fourth of July rocket. How she missed him!

The light was on in the booth. Someone was in there. Karen hated eavesdropping on other peoples' conversations, but the next phone was four blocks away. She had to wait. Making herself unobtrusive, she bent down and retied her shoelace. A man's overcoat stuck out of the folding door, leaving it ajar.

"— somebody has to teach you a lesson," the man was saying. His gloved hand clenched the receiver in a grip so tight, the leather wrinkled.

Karen rocked back on her heels slightly to look into the booth. The man hadn't noticed her, his back was to her. But then he half-turned and she could see his face in the bluish-white florescent light.

He looked familiar. She racked her brain. Wasn't he somebody who worked with her father at the mill? That was it — she couldn't remember his name, but vaguely recalled her father mentioning that this guy drifted into Chrystal Falls last winter, looking for work.

He was assigned a position on her father's shift, so undoubtedly he was laid off when everyone else was.

Karen melted into the shadows. He still hadn't seen her and suddenly she didn't want him to know she was there. He laughed into the receiver, a sinister, unmirthful sound.

"— too late. Bye-bye, Chels. Be seeing you around."

He hung up, slammed open the folding door, and left, hurrying up "A" Avenue as if he had an important appointment.

From her hiding place in the shadows, Karen watched him until he was gone from sight, her heart in her throat. "Bye-bye, Chels," he'd said! Who else was nicknamed Chels — no one but Chelsea Chrystal! And what was the last thing he said?

Be seeing you around!

She went into the phone booth. A piece of paper on the floor caught her eye. She picked it up. A jagged scrawl spelled out an address and phone number. Karen didn't recognize the number but she'd know that understated, elegant address anywhere. Chelsea's address.

This was the man making threatening phone calls to Chelsea. It had to be! So Chelsea wasn't crying wolf the other day in gym class.

He definitely appeared unhinged. Karen wondered if losing his job had pushed him over the edge and was thankful her own father made the best of a bad situation. Where was that guy going now, after telling Chelsea he'd see her around? To teach her a lesson, as he'd implied?

Chelsea craved excitement, but not this kind. This man was obviously deranged. He might hurt her. Someone had to stop him, and she was the only person who knew his identity. A thought twisted through Karen's brain. Why should she bother to help Chelsea? What had Chelsea ever done for her?

For once, maybe Chelsea ought to get what she deserved.

Chapter Fourteen.

Karen leaned against the phone booth for support. Beneath her jacket, the glass walls felt cold. For the first time in her life, she understood the phrase "caught on the horns of a dilemma," as needlelike jabs prodded her conscience.

Here, practically in the palm of her hand, was the chance to even the score between her and Chelsea Chrystal. If she wanted, she could toss away the incriminating scrap of paper with Chelsea's address and phone number and forget she even walked in this direction tonight, much less overheard a threatening phone call. Wasn't it time a Chrystal suffered a little? After all, milltowners had been paying for the pleasures of the rich Hill people ever since the first Chrystal cast his lofty glance over the valley and decreed, "I will live up *here* and *they* will live down *there*."

Aside from ancient grievances, Karen's own

life had been turned upside-down by Chrystals. First there was the hit-and-run accident in which Mitch had been implicated — the flimsy evidence against him fanned into a full-blown fire by Hill people, impatient to place the blame on a milltowner. On the heels of that ugly business came the layoff at the mill, putting her father out of work, followed by the shocking discovery of her mother's affair with Chelsea's father, who had rejected her years ago. Insult piled upon insult. Was it any wonder she hated Chelsea's family?

And Chelsea herself — the golden princess of Chrystal Falls. She had it all, clothes, a mansion and servants, fancy cars, grandparents who spoiled her rotten, a wonderful future shining before her. If someone asked Chelsea the definition of hardship, she'd have to look it up in the dictionary.

Karen's education, on the other hand, began early. She never forgot that day when she enviously watched the magic yellow school bus on its way to pick up the rich kids and take them to their special elementary school, experiencing the bitter taste of inequality. The word "unfair" wasn't on any of her first grade vocabulary lists, but Karen learned its meaning nonetheless.

Chelsea represented the uneven scales that tipped in favor of the Hill: Whatever Chelsea had, Karen didn't, and probably never would have as long as the Chrystals ran the town.

And now Karen had the chance to see Chelsea suffer, for a change. She savored the image.

The wind ruffled the slip of paper in her fingers. She looked at Chelsea's address again, craggy letters forming spiteful peaks, t's and i's dashed and dotted with an angry pen. This was the handwriting of a disturbed person. The words he spoke into the phone were no joke — he was deadly serious. Chelsea Chrystal was in real danger.

Karen remembered Chelsea's expression in the locker room, when she confided to Dawn and Karen that someone was after her. The pupils of her blue eyes were dilated with fear, and lines of anxiety bracketed her mouth. Much as she disliked Chelsea, much as she wanted revenge against the Chrystals, Karen knew she would never forgive herself if she was responsible for something awful happening to another human being. Something she could have prevented.

Time was running out. That man was undoubtedly on his way to Chelsea's, bent on "teaching her a lesson," whatever that was. He might even be there by now. She had to take action, fast. Digging for change in her jacket pocket, Karen grabbed the receiver of the phone. As she fed money into the slot, another thought struck her. She had to do more than just make a phone call.

She dialed the number of the garage where Mitch worked. When Pete Carter answered, his voice nearly drowned out by clangs and shouts in the background, Karen thought for a moment she had dialed the wrong number. Of course she knew that Pete worked as a mechanic there, too; he had helped Mitch get a position at the garage. She was too distraught to think clearly.

"Pete, it's Karen. Is Mitch around?"

"He's on break," Pete replied. "I'll get him."

Karen gnawed at a fingernail while she waited. The slip of paper rested on the ledge from which ripped phone directories dangled. Hurry, Mitch, she implored silently.

At last he came on the line. "Hi, babe. What's up?"

"Can you get away from work? Chelsea Chrystal's in real trouble. I need to get up to her house right away."

He responded to the urgency in her tone, not wasting time. "Where are you?"

"A and Broad. Next to the bookstore."

"Don't move," he instructed. "Be there in five minutes."

Karen's teeth began to chatter. She felt icy with fear. Where was that man now? Had he reached the Chrystal mansion? It seemed unlikely, since he'd scuttled down the street on foot. But maybe he had left his car a block away. This tedious waiting was driving her crazy.

She dropped her last quarter into the slot and dialed Dawn's number. Dawn would want to know what was going on. After all, Chelsea had told Dawn about the calls in the locker room the other day.

Dawn answered on the second ring, her hello a little flustered.

"Dawn? It's Karen."

"Karen?" She sounded surprised, as if she had been expecting someone else. "Hi. I thought it might be —" She didn't have to finish. Karen suspected the "someone" was Pete Carter.

"Listen, Dawn. I don't have much time. I saw that man who's been bothering Chelsea. He's after her, right this minute. Mitch is coming to get me and we're going up there to warn Chelsea."

"My God, Karen! She was right! And we almost didn't believe her. I want to go, too, only I'm not sure if Josh has the car —"

A screech of rubber told Karen Mitch had arrived. "I can't talk anymore. Mitch is here."

"Then go! I'll get there somehow. Karen, hurry!"

"Yes, young lady? Can I help you?" Alexander Chrystal was framed by imposing double doors, a pair of reading glasses perched halfway down his nose. He didn't look at all like a man who secretly met other men's wives.

"It's Chelsea," Karen blurted out. "Is she okay? There's a man — I think he's coming after her!"

"Chelsea's in her room . . . what on earth are you talking about? Do I know you?" He scrutinized her over his glasses, then recognition lit his eyes.

"I'm Karen Pickett —"

"Pickett," he said wonderingly. "Gloria's

175

daughter. You're the spitting image."

Karen had no time to discuss family resemblances. It was all she could do to stand on the doorstep of this man's home. "I go to school with Chelsea," she stated bluntly. "She's been getting these calls and tonight — a little while ago — I saw the man in a phone booth."

He frowned. "Calls? What calls? Chelsea hasn't said anything —"

Would he ever let her finish? "She hasn't told you about them. She only mentioned it to Dawn Newhouse and me the other day. Mr. Chrystal, this man — I heard him say some nasty things to Chelsea. He dropped this." Karen handed the scrap to Alexander Chrystal. He pushed up his reading glasses and scanned the paper.

"I see," he said, but Karen knew he didn't see at all. "Come in — Karen. I'll get Chelsea and make sure she's all right. Then —"

"You don't understand, Mr. Chrystal. My boyfriend and I passed the man driving over here. He's on his way up here right now. You'd better call the police and have him picked up!"

Alexander left her standing in the foyer to run down the hall, calling his daughter. When he came back, Chelsea was with him, her cheeks streaked with tears and makeup. She wore a terrycloth bathrobe as though she was getting ready for bed, but her shoulders sagged with something weightier than end-of-the-day fatigue.

"Karen," Chelsea said weakly. "What are you doing here?"

"I saw him, Chelsea. I saw the man who's been bothering you. I came over to warn you." Despite the seriousness of the situation, Karen felt overcome with shyness, standing in the magnificent foyer of the Chrystal mansion for the first time.

"Oh, no," Chelsea wailed. "He just called again. He's after me!"

"I know," Karen told her. "I heard him myself."

"Daddy, call the police! Quick!"

"Just a minute, Chelsea. Come into my study," Alexander ordered Karen. "Before I call anyone, I have to get to the bottom of this."

Chelsea sat on the edge of a leather wing chair, shuddering as she recounted the nightly phone calls that had terrorized her for the past few weeks. When Mr. Chrystal turned to Karen, she repeated her side of the story, explaining how she overheard the man in the phone booth and found the paper.

"So I called Mitch — he's my boyfriend — at the garage where he works and asked him to drive me up here. On the way over, we saw the man walking up the road," she concluded.

"Who is this man?" Alexander asked his daughter.

Chelsea shook her head. "I don't know. He's never said — though he did mention something about the mill tonight."

Karen cut in. "I know who he is, sort of. He used to work with my father. They were on the same shift. I remember Daddy telling me once this man drifted into town last year looking for work. I forgot his name but he was laid off when my father was," she added emphatically. "I think losing his job made him — well, unbalanced."

Alexander needed to hear no more. He snatched the phone on his desk and punched the buttons with brisk authority. "This is Alexander Chrystal. I need a police officer up here immediately," he said in a tone guaranteed to stifle any argument on the other end. "My daughter has been harassed by some vagrant. You'll find him on the road . . . yes, on foot. Possibly dangerous."

Minutes later, they learned that a man answering to Karen's description had been picked up at the foot of the Chrystals' driveway. He was unarmed and disoriented.

"As soon as they get that man into custody, the captain is sending someone over to question you girls," Alexander reported to them. "I'd like a little more information myself, before he gets here."

"I don't know any more," Karen said defensively. "Just what I told you and that's all."

"I believe you," Mr. Chrystal reassured her. "It's Chelsea I need to talk to." He came from behind his desk and asked his daughter, "You've been getting these calls for weeks, apparently. Why didn't you come to me before now? When it was almost too late?"

Chelsea dug her toe into the lush pile of the blue and gold carpet. Hunched in the loose-fitting bathrobe, mascara tracks drying on her cheeks, she seemed more like a bedraggled child than princess of the Hill. Tremors rippled across her shoulders, as if she couldn't stop thinking about that last frightening phone call . . . and how close she had come to being hurt.

Karen felt a twinge of sympathy for her. The princess had lost her crown. Chelsea appeared subdued, beaten — a look Karen never thought she'd ever see marring the perfect features of a Chrystal.

"I'm waiting, Chelsea." Mr. Chrystal removed his glasses and tapped them against his palm.

"I — it's personal," Chelsea mumbled finally. "Do I have to tell you — in front of her?"

Karen's temper erupted. "I come all the way up here to save your ungrateful hide and you don't want to talk to your father in front of me! What about *me*? How do you think *I* feel?" Addressing Alexander Chrystal, Karen said, "I know why Chelsea never told you about the calls. She couldn't trust you anymore — not after she found out you were sneaking around to see my mother!"

Karen expected Mr. Chrystal to deny it. In fact, she desperately hoped he would. But instead he merely sighed, an open admission of guilt.

"So that's it," he said, more to himself than

to either Chelsea or Karen. "Gloria and I . . . it was a long time ago."

"No, it wasn't," Karen argued. "You were with my mother only last week. I saw you both in that coffee shop on West Street."

"Is that true?" Chelsea covered her face with her hands. "Oh, God, it gets worse."

Alexander was clearly agitated. "Chelsea . . . Karen. Both of you, *listen* to me. Yes, I did see Gloria the other day. We bumped into each other and decided to have a cup of coffee. For old time's sake." He sketched an apologetic gesture. "I'm sorry if I caused you any grief, Karen. But there is nothing between your mother and me. We are simply old friends."

"Old friends!" Karen hurled his words back at him. "You were more than friends with her. She told me you wanted to marry her, but your family said she wasn't good enough for you, so you left her. Is that the way you treat your friends?"

"Daddy!" Chelsea cried, astonished. "You were actually going to *marry* Karen's mother? How could you do that to Mother?"

He waved away their exclamations. "This is getting out of hand. You don't know what you're talking about, either of you. The truth is, Karen . . . Chelsea, that I met Gloria White long before I met Elizabeth. And before Gloria met Carl Pickett, I might add."

"Is it true you asked her to marry you?" Karen pressed.

"Yes, I did. And I wanted to marry Gloria.

But we were both young," he qualified. "Still in high school. Did we really know what we wanted at that age?"

Karen exchanged a meaningful glance with Chelsea. They were both sixteen, in high school. Karen knew what she wanted out of life and she suspected Chelsea did, too.

"Did you leave Karen's mother?" Chelsea asked, her voice quavering with apprehension.

"Don't put it that way," her father said. "Life is not black and white, you know. We broke up — rather, I broke up with Gloria, which sounds like I left her. But it was a mutual decision, you both must understand. True, my parents did not approve of Gloria, but that wasn't the only reason we parted company. Gloria wasn't sure she wanted me, wasn't sure she could face life in this house."

Karen had no difficulty believing that. Now she knew what her mother had meant when she said she'd glimpsed life on the Hill and decided it wasn't for her. The Chrystal mansion was beautiful, certainly, but it was also formidable. To Karen it was an elegant palace without one glimmer of the warmth that radiated from the Pickett house. Her mother made their house a home — an impossible task in this marble mansion.

"You see, girls," Alexander went on, "we were both changing, ju as you two are changing every day. We weren't ready to face marriage and we realized it."

"My mother still has the pin you gave her," Karen said impulsively.

A ghost of a smile flitted across Alexander's solemn features, sadly reminiscent. "Does she really? I'm glad."

"Does Mother know about this?" Chelsea asked, still unaccepting.

"Of course," her father replied. "She's always known about Gloria. And Carl has always known about me, I'm sure. Gloria never could stand a shred of dishonesty. That was one of the things I liked about her."

Karen allowed her gaze to drift around the study. Mr. Chrystal's home office was like a room she'd expect to find in the state capital, it was that imposing. Bookshelves built into the walnut paneling held thick volumes bound in leather. Framed hunting prints hanging over the marble fireplace lent a hint of outdoorsy sophistication to the stolid furnishings, as did the wooden decoy ducks and the pair of brass quails squatting on the mantle. Alexander's desk, a massive piece of furniture, stood before a pair of rich leather chairs. Near the tall, many-paned windows, an antique globe waited for idle fingers to spin it with a single touch, perhaps to choose the next glamorous vacation spot.

Outside, headlights suddenly glared across the windows.

"The police are here," Alexander said. "Karen, I think you should call your parents and let them know where you are. You'll probably be here a while longer." He pushed the phone toward her. "Oh, yes. Tell your father that after Thanksgiving, we're putting the workers back into the mill on a part-time basis. I expect the mill will be fully operational by the first of the year." He stared pointedly at his daughter. "Chelsea, don't you have anything to say to Karen?"

Karen could barely hear Chelsea as she murmured, "Thanks, Karen. Thanks for — believing me."

She met Chelsea's eyes. A flicker of understanding passed between them. They had both felt betrayed by their parents; both had experienced the suffocating sensation of being the object of malicious gossip. Both had been caught up in a love affair that was older than they were, but still had the intensity to transcend time and entangle them in its intricate web.

Yet they remained poles apart: Chelsea, high on her Hill with her easy lifestyle; and Karen buried below in milltown, waiting for the chance to break free.

Karen knew that the alliance between Hill and Mill was only temporary — a fleeting, uneasy truce. Some things never changed.

"I'll call my folks in a minute," Karen said. "I'd like to go tell Mitch what's happening. He's out in the car."

"Ask him in," Mr. Chrystal offered. "I'll have Marie make a pot of coffee. I think we can all use a cup. I know I can."

"Thanks, but I doubt he'll come in," Karen said. "He's kind of shy." Mitch would probably feel as overwhelmed and out of place as she did. She let herself out the front door and ran down the stone-flagged path to Mitch's car. He was leaning against the hood.

"You were in there so long, I started to worry," he told her. "Is Chelsea all right?"

"She's okay." Karen was explaining the situation to Mitch when two cars, one behind the other, rolled up the driveway. The first was a squad car and a uniformed policeman got out and strode up to the door.

The second vehicle, a silver Honda Karen didn't recognize, pulled up beside them. Dawn leaped from the driver's side, her glossy black hair in disarray.

"Karen — Mitch! I got here as soon as I could. I borrowed a car from the lady in the next apartment. How's Chelsea?"

"She's fine. Or at least she will be, when this is all over," Karen replied. "The police caught the guy. I have to go back inside for questioning myself. She'll be glad you came, Dawn," she added, remembering how forlorn and alone Chelsea looked when her father called her from her room.

Mitch put his arm around her shoulder, as he stared at the mansion. "It's a big house, isn't it?"

"Yes." Too big, Karen thought, comparing the cool, beautifully-furnished rooms to the warm, cozy clutter of her own house. A white blur was pressed to the window of the study an instant, then gone. Was that Chelsea, watching them? "Money isn't everything," she said to no one in particular.

"That's for sure," Dawn agreed. "All the

money in the world couldn't protect Chelsea from that man." A bitter wind sprang up, reminding them that December was only a breath away. "I guess we'd better go in."

"You know," Karen mused aloud. "I almost feel sorry for her."

"Me, too," Dawn whispered.

Karen hoped the police officer wouldn't detain her much longer. Suddenly she wanted to get home, out of the cold.

Dawn put an arm around Karen's shoulders and they walked up to the house. Dawn, too, wanted to leave quickly and get to Pete. To tell him what Karen had said. "Money isn't everything."

Would Pete believe it?

When heartless Monty Chrystal comes home, Dawn is not ready for her feelings. Read Chrystal Falls #3, THE BAD AND THE BEAUTIFUL.

Announcing a Hot New Series!

COUPLES™

You'll fall in LOVE!

Is there really someone for everyone? YES! Read about those special moments, those tentative steps towards first love...finding each other, getting together, breaking up, making up. **A NEW BOOK EACH MONTH.** That's **COUPLES™**: stories of dreams come true!

Phoebe and Brad. For two years, they thought they were in love. But along comes dreamy Griffin, an aspiring actor—and Phoebe's falling again!

Chris and Ted. Problems with her stepsister Brenda get popular Chris so crazy, she almost loses her football-star boyfriend...*and* her best friend Phoebe.

Brenda. When the going gets tough, she turns to her loving friends at the halfway house. Nobody understands...except for one special guy.

Laurie. Spoiled and snobbish, Laurie's used to having her own way. Will she get unsuspecting Peter, the handsome but aloof D.J.?

Woody. Friendly, sensitive and artistic, he's got everything going for him—except the girl.

Janie. Maybe she hasn't got a chance with Peter. But this "plain Jane" *will* have a chance at love!

Book #4	Look for #5
Made For Each Other	**Moving Too Fast**
at your bookstore now! $2.50	coming in October 1985

COU 854   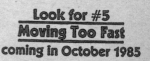 Scholastic Books

CHEERLEADERS™

Join the Team!

They're talented. They're fabulous-looking. They're winners! And they've got what you want! Don't miss any of these exciting CHEERLEADERS books!

Watch for these titles! $2.25 each

- ☐ QI 33402-6 **Trying Out** *Caroline B. Cooney*
- ☐ QI 33403-4 **Getting Even** *Christopher Pike*
- ☐ QI 33404-2 **Rumors** *Caroline B. Cooney*
- ☐ QI 33405-0 **Feuding** *Lisa Norby*
- ☐ QI 33406-9 **All the Way** *Caroline B. Cooney*
- ☐ QI 33407-7 **Splitting** *Jennifer Sarasin*
